Paperback edition 2022

Kindle edition 2022

Paperback ISBN: 9798849416496

Cover Design: Author

FOR DAD, LOVE YOU ALWAYS X

VOLANS

Around Chris pandemonium was breaking out. Voices were calling for him to be removed, for the dragon to be forced to find a different partner, or worse. The noise and confusion in the cave roused Taivas. Not usually protective of their young once they were hatched, she hadn't been taking any notice of the humans, until they began threatening her offspring. She almost ran towards the seating and reared up, wings spread wide, as she bellowed her fury at the angry people.

Fallaren was calling to other riders to come forward. Nat and Dar came leaping down the steps, calling to their friends to join them.

Without his noticing it, Chris was surrounded by a protective ring. The riders stood with their backs to Chris and the baby dragon, facing the crowds. Fallaren was speaking urgently to Narilka and casting worried looks at Chris, who was oblivious.

CHAPTER 1

Chris looked up, his eyes sparkling. He was amazed to find himself looking at the backs of several rider's heads. He sought Jay and Anilla, caught their worried looks, and realised just what he'd done. The dragon bumped him with his nose, demanding attention from his chosen one. Chris returned his gaze to the beautiful creature before him, but now with the realisation of what had happened and how challenging his life at Portum was about to become.

'Just as I'd started to settle in too!' he said softly.

He could hear Fallaren talking loudly to someone who kept shouting.

'...needs to be taken away. This can't be allowed,' he heard the man shout.

'There is no need for that,' Fallaren said, 'the young man may not have been here for long but he has proved himself...'

'He's not been here long enough to become a rider!' the strident voice continued, determined to hold sway.

'The choice, if there is one to be made, is for Fallaren and myself. It is not open for debate!' That was Narilka, Chris had only heard her sound so angry once before, he almost felt sorry for whoever she was directing her fury at.

'But,' the shouter carried on, 'my boy was left standing and that…that beast walked straight past him!'

'It is always the dragon's choice.' Narilka's voice cracked, whip-like.

'Your son was unlucky this time, like so many others,' Fallaren said, his voice was conciliatory now, 'but there will be more clutches and that will give time for Timeon to pass his journeyman's exams, won't it?'

The shouter humphed but wisely chose to stop arguing.

People were leaving now, the crowds were thinning. Still Chris was surrounded by his guard of riders. He was aware that some folk were looking at him angrily as they passed, but what could he do? He kept his attention on the dragon, whose colour was showing now as his hide dried. The deep bronze came as a shock, he didn't think he'd seen a bronze dragon while he'd been here, not that he'd seen many at all, but mostly they seemed to be blue or green, with the odd silvery white one, and one that glittered like gold in the sunlight.

The young dragon told Chris he was very hungry; images of food and a sudden hunger came over Chris. Looking around he spotted Nat and tapped her on the shoulder.

'Excuse me,' he said quietly, 'but he's hungry. How long till I can get him something to eat?'

'Won't be long now Midget,' Nat replied, giving him a quick wink over her shoulder, 'Fallaren's sorting this lot out,' she indicated the people leaving the cave. He noticed for the first time that riders were escorting them, ensuring an orderly, swift exit.

Then, quite suddenly, the cave was empty of spectators.

'Thank you,' Fallaren said to the riders guarding Chris and the dragon, 'You may go now, I think we need to get this young man and his dragon something to eat.'

Chris looked relieved and urged his dragon to follow Fallaren and Narilka to the back of the cave where he could now see other hatchlings gathered.

'Chris, this is Remnac, he's one of our senior riders. It's his responsibility to look after all our new riders and dragons,' Fallaren said.

'Hello Chris,' Remnac said, looking closely at him. He handed Chris a bucket full of meat scraps. The dragon immediately tried to put his head in the bucket, but Remnac jerked it out of his reach.

'Like this,' Remnac took a couple of pieces of meat from the bucket and offered them to the dragon, who gulped them down and looked for more. 'They're always like this at first,' he said with a laugh, 'if we're not careful with them, they'll choke themselves on their food.'

Chris nodded, watching closely, 'How long will this stage last?' he asked.

'Around three months,' Remnac said, handing the bucket back to Chris, 'Prepare yourself for a busy time young man. Lots for you to learn.' He turned from Chris and moved among the dragons now, checking them all.

'Well, young Chris, you're a surprise, aren't you?' Chris turned to find Narilka standing beside him. 'May

I?' she took meat from the bucket and offered it to the dragon, who snatched it from her fingers. 'What's his name?' she asked.

'Name? I have no idea,' Chris said, 'How do I name a dragon?'

'You don't,' Narilka was laughing at him now, 'They already have a name. Hasn't he told you yet? Naughty boy, we'll have to keep an eye on you.' She patted the baby affectionately and gave him more meat.

Chris fed the dragon some more, looking thoughtfully at him. 'So, what is your name dragon?' he asked. The dragon swallowed a large lump of meat without chewing and looked at his rider, eyes whirling. 'Hessarion?' Chris said slowly, 'have I got that right?' The dragon butted against him, demanding more food. Chris gave in, fishing a large chunk of meat from the bucket for him, 'chew it this time.'

'Hessarion?' Narilka said, 'I like it! Now Chris, I don't know how much you heard of what was going on after young Hess here chose you, but you stirred up a hornet's nest.' She saw Chris's bewildered face and shook her head, 'This is why we prefer folk to have lived in Portum for at least a year before they try for a dragon,' she said, 'you're still learning to be outside, learning our ways, our culture. However,' she said with a sigh, 'you were chosen and we all have to deal with it, despite the anger of some and the disappointment of others. Fallaren is likely to call a meeting in the morning, and your presence will be required.'

Chris felt his stomach drop as she spoke but nodded mutely. He'd ruined everything, his new life was in tatters before it had really begun.

CHAPTER 2

The morning after the hatching, Chris awoke to a soft nose insistently nudging him. Hess was awake and he was hungry. Chris heard his tummy rumbling and, laughing, pushed him away.

'Let me get dressed,' he said, 'then we can find you some breakfast.'

Hess reluctantly climbed down off the bed and sat, watching Chris closely as he grabbed his clothes. Shoving his legs into his trousers and hurriedly pulling on his shirt, Chris looked around. He was in a big dormitory where all the new riders and their young dragons slept. They would be here for at least three months. Around him other riders were being woken by their dragons and there was much sleepy protesting.

Chris and Hess were first to make their way towards the area designated for feeding. They'd been given a whistle-stop tour of their new accommodation the previous evening, but Chris was a little vague. It had all happened so quickly. Remnac was waiting at the feeding area. He nodded good morning to Chris and handed him a bucket, pointing to the first bay. Hess followed Chris and the bucket to the area, enclosed on three sides by rough walls. This was to reduce stress and food envy among the young dragons. Fights, he had been told, used to be regular occurrences before the partitions had been installed.

Chris focussed on Hess and began offering him pieces of meat. By the time they were halfway through their bucket he could hear others arriving and gradually the bays filled with hungry young dragons and their rookie riders.

Once Hess had eaten all his food he sat, burping happily if none too gently, while Chris returned the bucket and looked for Remnac.

'What do I do now?' Chris asked.

'Morning bath time,' Remnac grinned, 'if you can keep him awake long enough that is!'

Chris glanced over his shoulder to see a sleepy Hess leaning against the wall, his eyes closing.

'Take him down to the bathing room. I showed you where it is last night, didn't I?' Chris nodded, hoping he could remember. 'I'll be along in a minute or two, but you can get him into the pool at least. OK?'

'Ok,' Chris turned to Hess, 'come on lazy bones, bath time.'

A grumbling Hess followed his new friend down the passage and into the dragon's bathroom. There was a large, shallow pool in the middle of the floor surrounded by several small platforms which were for the young dragons to stand on whilst they were being scrubbed and cleaned.

'Off you go,' he said, 'into the water, enjoy it while it's nice and quiet in here.'

Hess reluctantly waded into the water, splashing

with his tail to show his disapproval.

'Now you get yourself good and wet all over,' Chris instructed, 'then we can get you all nice and clean.'

Remnac arrived as Chris was issuing his instructions and he laughed as Hess submerged himself in the centre of the pool and blew bubbles.

'He's going to be a handful, that one,' he said to Chris. 'You got enough sand? Know what you're doing?'

Chris looked confused, 'Sand?' he queried.

'Ah yes, you haven't had the training, have you? Alright I'll give you a quick run through. Once your dragon is done messing about in the water,' they both looked at Hess who was now wallowing happily, 'you persuade him out and onto this platform. Then you take handfuls of this soft sand,' he demonstrated, taking up a handful from the large box beside the platform, 'and you rub him all over. It's really important to look after his hide, these babies grow so quickly their skins can hardly keep up and it's better to prevent problems than save up trouble for later. After you've scrubbed him, he can go and rinse himself off. Good idea for you to go in with him and make sure he gets all the sand off him.'

Chris, who had been listening intently, looked worried. 'Go in the water with him?' he asked, 'I really don't like water.'

'Oh you'll be fine,' Remnac said airily, 'it's not deep, look, he can stand up in the middle. We just need you to make sure he's got all the sand off him; it foams when it gets wet so it's not hard. Once he's rinsed off, we'll get to the next stage. Hope you're fit, lad, looking after one of these is hard work!' with a grin Remnac turned to the next new pair and instructed them.

'Ok then,' Chris said under his breath, 'we can do this. Come on Hess, out you come.' Hess rolled over in the water, splashing and playing. 'Hessarion! Get out of there now.' Chris tried to sound stern. Hess ignored him. Chris sat down on the platform, 'Fine then, stay in there, don't get nice and clean so you can go for a snooze. See if I care.' Chris turned slightly away from the pool and watched other riders encouraging their dragons into the water. Out of the corner of his eye he saw Hess begin making his way towards the platform. Hiding a smile, Chris stood up and made much of taking his shoes off, setting them neatly near the wall. When he turned around, Hess was standing on the platform.

'Ah, there you are. Ready?' Hess settled down and Chris scooped up handfuls of sand and began rubbing it onto the dragon. It quickly became clear that this was going to be a messy business. A flapping, wet dragon and strange, foaming sand coupled with Chris's lack of experience meant that he was soon soaking wet and there were foamy, sandy puddles everywhere.

Satisfied at long last that he had covered every inch of hide with sand, Chris sent Hess back into the pool to rinse himself off. As he plucked up the courage to step into the water himself, Chris glanced around at the rest of his 'class' and noticed, with some relief, that they were all experiencing similar issues.

Taking a deep breath, he stepped off the edge of the pool and into the water, which lapped round his calves as Hess and a couple of other dragons wallowed enthusiastically. Slowly he made his way over to his dragon. As he waded the water gradually crept up his thighs, and by the time he made it to Hess it was at hip level and Chris was starting to panic. Hess showed no concern whatsoever, rolling around in the water and playing with his clutch mates.

'Come here,' Chris said, 'let me make sure you're properly cleaned off now.'

Hess looked at Chris and seemed to be considering what to do before, slowly and with obvious reluctance, he made his way to his friend and allowed him to inspect him for clinging sand. When none was found Chris told him to go back to the platform. They waded towards the edge of the pool together, Hess bumping against Chris playfully and almost knocking him off his feet a couple of times. Chris had to catch hold of Hess's shoulders to keep himself from falling.

'Stop that!' he said firmly, wondering if the dragon could feel his nerves.

They made it to the edge of the pool with no further incidents and Hess climbed onto the cleaning station, giving his wings a good shake as he did so, scattering droplets of water and showering Chris. Then he settled down to wait.

Chris shook the water out of his eyes and looked around. Everyone seemed to be at different stages of the bathing process, a couple were still sanding their dragons, some were playing in the water with theirs. Remnac was standing over the smallest dragon and his rider, demonstrating the correct way to apply sand. The dragon kept squirming to look at what was happening.

Chris sat with a sigh on the edge of the platform and leaned against Hess. The dragon squeaked happily and curved his neck round to look at his rider. Absently, Chris reached up and stroked the nose. Hess flicked his tongue out and licked Chris's cheek, then he settled down and seemed to be nodding off.

'You with the bronze,' Remnac's voice carried across the noise from the pool, making Chris jump, 'Come and get your oil please.'

Oil? Chris had no idea what to expect, but he trotted over to Remnac and was handed a stone jug.

'You pour some onto your hands and you rub it into your dragon's hide,' Remnac told him, 'And do try to keep him awake!'

Chris glanced across to where Hess was settled, eyes closed. He grinned at Remnac, 'I'll try,' he said, 'but he doesn't seem too keen.'

'They're always like this at first,' Remnac said, 'but oil first, nap later. Off you go.'

Chris made his way back to Hess, aware of others watching him. He looked around and nodded, smiling at his fellow new riders, but he was met with suspicious looks and, from one boy, open anger. Frowning he looked away and walked to Hess.

'Come on sleepy,' he said, pushing at the hind quarters of the tired dragon, 'I've got to oil you now, then you can go for a snooze if you like.'

Hess shuffled a little but made no effort to stand up so Chris unstoppered the jug and poured some oil onto his hands. Then, with smooth strokes, he began applying the oil to the bits of his dragon that he could reach. Hess shifted some more until he was sitting up, allowing Chris to apply the soothing oil to his soft underbelly.

'Now, do I oil your wings too?' Chris wondered, stroking oil onto a foreleg. He looked up to see Remnac watching the girl next to him as she carefully oiled her dragon's neck. 'Er, Remnac?' he said, 'sorry to interrupt.'

'Then don't!' snapped the girl.

Chris and Remnac looked shocked, but Remnac turned to Chris, 'no trouble lad,' he said, 'what's the matter?'

'I was just wondering if we're supposed to oil the wings too?' Chris said, looking wonderingly from Remnac to the girl and back again.

'Yes, you can give the wings a coating,' Remnac said to him, 'it's better to be thorough. Well done.' Then he returned his attention to the girl, showing her where she'd missed a bit. 'We're all tired and stressed Tammy,' he said to her, 'no need for that attitude. This young man is in the same position as you.'

Chris couldn't hear her reply, so he concentrated on oiling wings, which was a tricky job made trickier by Hess not wanting to keep still. After the third time of being smacked round the face by an oily wing Chris gave up and went round the other side to attend to the second wing.

'Keep still Hess,' he said as the dragon wriggled, 'if you keep still, I can do this so much faster.' Hess seemed to be trying and the second wing took much less time than the first.

Once he was sure he'd done, Chris put the stopper back in the jug and took it back to the table Remnac had taken if from. Unsure what to do next, he looked around. Everyone seemed to be onto oiling their dragons now, some were having more trouble than others. As he watched there was a crash as one dragon pushed the jug over and an oil slick covered the platform and his rider, who was wailing in despair.

'When you're done,' Remnac's voice rose above the chaos, 'you can take your dragons back to their beds. They'll sleep a lot these first few weeks, enjoy it while you can. Then you can go along and get your breakfasts, you deserve it!' He gave a laugh that sounded to Chris like a bark.

Chris urged Hess from the platform and the pair headed back to the dormitory. Once there, Hess made himself comfortable on his stone bed, which Remnac had said was called a couch, and within minutes he was fast asleep. Just the tip of his tail twitched. Chris gently patted the end of his nose, then made his way to the dining area for his breakfast. It was quite a while before his classmates joined him, by this time he was on his second plate of food.

He had expected them all to sit together, but the other new riders all chose to sit at different tables and Chris was left alone. He felt a little unsure about this but carried on eating. He was going to need all his strength, he was sure. He was finishing his batu when Remnac appeared.

'All eaten? Good.' He looked around the room, frowning when he spotted Chris sat alone. 'Go wash and change, then we move on to lessons,' he said to the group, 'all except for you, that is.' He pointed at Chris, 'You, young man, have to make yourself presentable and go see

Fallaren, he's called a meeting of the Council and your presence is required.'

Chris felt himself burning as all eyes turned on him. He nodded mutely and stood up, stacking his dishes and taking them to the counter on his way out.

CHAPTER 3

In the council chamber, Fallaren was addressing the assembled leaders when Chris arrived. He loitered outside the door, unsure, nervous of his reception. Anilla spotted him as she was on her way to work and she hurried over.

'What are you doing here?' she whispered.

'I...er...Remnac said there was a meeting and I was required to attend.'

'You best go in then,' she said, 'I'm sure it'll be ok, Fallaren had your back last night, but you certainly caused a stir!'

'But,' Chris stalled, 'what are they going to do to me? What can they do to me?'

Anilla shrugged, 'Nothing too terrible, now stop being silly and get in there.' Shaking her head, Anilla gave a loud knock on the chamber door and, grinning unrepentantly at Chris, she turned and walked quickly away.

There was a sudden silence in the chamber and the door creaked open, revealing Narilka's face. She looked relieved to see Chris.

'Oh, it's you Chris, come in.' She held the door open wider and ushered him into the large chamber.

Chris had never seen the council in session before, the huge table was crowded with craft masters and senior members of the Portum community. He recognised the Smith master, and several other senior craft members, then he felt a shot of relief as he spotted Garad.

Fallaren was on his feet and looking annoyed. He gave Chris a brief flash of a smile before waving him to a seat directly next to him, to the right. Chris made his way round the table, aware of the looks he was getting as he did so.

'Welcome Chris,' Fallaren said, putting a hand on his shoulder as Chris sat beside him, 'this meeting has been called because of what happened last night.'

'I'm sorry,' Chris said quietly, 'I never meant...'

'You have nothing to be sorry for young man!' Fallaren sounded angry now, 'if you hadn't been there, that young dragon would have remained riderless, and we all know how that ends.' He glared around the table, challenging those present to argue.

'It's not right,' said a man with a high, whiny voice, 'he's not been here five minutes, he shouldn't be allowed to become a rider. I say the dragon should be taken away from him.'

'And what, Master Rampton, do you suggest we do with the beast?' Narilka's eyes were sparkling with anger as she spoke.

Rampton shrugged, 'What usually happens to dragons when you do that?'

'Nothing,' Narilka said, 'because it never happens. Once that bond is made it cannot be severed, except by the death of one of the pair. Are you suggesting that we kill a dragon?' She glared at the master, who Chris now recognised as one of the Tannery team.

Rampton shuffled uncomfortably and rubbed his chin, 'Well now, I'm not suggesting that at all,' he said, glancing at Chris and Fallaren then back to Narilka, 'but couldn't the beast be paired with someone else? Someone who has the right knowledge and experience? My son for example. He was there last night, but he was left standing, while this...this...lad,' Rampton managed to put a lot of spite into the word, 'walks away with a prize he doesn't deserve!'

'Who are you to say if he deserves his dragon or not?' Fallaren asked quietly. The menace in his tone was obvious to all around the table, except the one the comment was directed at.

'Well,' Rampton whined, 'I think we can safely say that our rules, which clearly state that no one can become a rider until they have lived among us for at least a year, have been broken. Surely the lad should be receiving punishment for his actions last night, not being given the opportunity to become a rider, with all the glory and privileges that go with it?'

'Dragons don't bond with another.' Narilka said sharply, 'Once the bond is formed, that's it. It cannot be broken and a new bond formed just to satisfy the whims of men.' Narilka put the same quality into the word men that Rampton had managed to put into lad.

Chris listened, horrified. Surely, they couldn't take Hess away from him and kill him? They wouldn't, would they? He thought of the warmth of the bond he shared with his dragon and knew that, if Rampton were allowed to have his way, he, Chris, would be forever damaged. He hung his head and sighed, trying desperately not to cry.

'Your son,' Fallaren said, 'can always try again at the next hatching, as I said to you last night, he can use this time to work on his journeyman pin. His efforts will not be wasted.'

'But who can say when the next clutch will be laid?' Rampton said, 'I say that lad should be punished and the dragon be taken from him.'

'No.' Chris shocked himself by speaking. 'You can't take Hess away from me, it would kill both of us. Look, I'm sorry, I certainly didn't plan what happened last night, but it did, and I don't see why Hess and I should be punished for something that isn't our fault. Sorry if I'm speaking out of turn,' he said to Fallaren, 'but I need you all to understand that, although I'm very new here, I've worked really hard to fit in and settle, and I'll continue to do so now that I have a dragon to look after. It's not going to be easy, but I don't have a choice. Hess depends on me now, and in time I'll depend on him, when we're flying with the others to protect you from the wilds.' He looked directly at Rampton, who refused to meet his gaze.

'Well said, young Chris,' Fallaren clapped him on the back so hard that Chris almost head butted the table. 'Chris didn't expect to go to his first ever hatching and come away with a dragon, he went purely to spectate, but things, and especially dragons, had their own agenda.'

He had hardly finished speaking when there was a loud knocking on the chamber door, followed almost immediately by the doors bursting open and a breathless messenger falling through them and staggering to the table.

The man leant on the table, bent double trying to catch his breath.

'What is the meaning of this?' Rampton began, snarling at the man, 'this is a council session, you have no business barging in here.'

'Eggs,' gasped the messenger.

'Eggs?' Narilka looked puzzled, 'What are you talking about man? The hatching was last night.'

'No, more eggs,' he panted, 'one of the queens, she's laying eggs.'

'Another clutch! Already?' Fallaren and Narilka shared a look which Chris didn't understand, surely this was a good thing, considering Rampton's insistence that his son should have a dragon.

'Thank you,' Fallaren said to the messenger, 'gentlemen,' he turned to address the startled assembly, 'it looks like we are going to be busy here in Portum. More dragons.' He nodded at Rampton, 'Your son may get his next chance sooner than any of us thought.'

Rampton was looking pleased, he shot an unpleasant look at Chris, 'At least my lad knows how we go on here,' he said, 'he won't need his hand holding.'

Chris could say nothing, he knew his knowledge was very patchy, but he was already learning. He hoped Remnac wouldn't get tired of him needing extra help.

The messenger was escorted from the chamber by Narilka, who could be heard calling for refreshments.

'I think we can call this meeting over gentlemen,' Fallaren said, 'I'm afraid I must ask you to leave, we have other issues which need to be dealt with this morning.'

With much muttering everyone around the table stood to leave. As they made their way to the door, one man stood alone at the table. Garad looked at Chris, then moved towards him.

'If I may say,' he said, putting an arm around Chris's shoulders, 'I am very proud of this young man. They,' he jerked his thumb at the retreating backs of the other masters, 'have no idea the amount of plain hard work involved in looking after a dragon, yet this youngster, ill prepared as he is, is willing to take it on. He's asked no questions, he's not moaned, he just gets on with the job. Edwin and I want you to know that we're delighted for you lad,' he gave the shocked Chris a squeeze, 'Don't take any notice of that lot, they're just jealous old fools.' He grinned at Fallaren, then, with a last shake of his apprentice's shoulders, he turned and left.

'You certainly make quite an impression,' Fallaren said to Chris after Garad had left, 'Narilka and I never thought we'd see those two accept anyone into their craft, but you and your young friend have worked miracles.' He gave Chris a grin, 'Don't worry about what other folk say, you got your dragon, Hess is it? You'll keep him. He chose you, never forget that. Now, if you'll excuse me, I need a word or several with Narilka.' He turned and walked away, leaving Chris standing alone in the council room.

He could keep Hess, stay with him and learn all about caring for him, riding him, not to mention fighting against the wild dragons. Relief and joy flooded him, knowing he had the backing of not only the leaders, but also his craft master. 'Yes!' the word escaped him in a jubilant hiss, 'I'll show them,' he said softly, 'I'll work harder than anyone else. Hess and I will prove ourselves.'

He walked the length of the chamber towards the huge double doors, as he did so he heard voices coming from the office. Narilka and Fallaren were talking.

'...no idea it would be so soon,' Narilka said, 'what are we to do Fallaren?'

'Do? Well, nothing we can do really love, the eggs will hatch,' he gave a nervous laugh.

'Don't be silly,' Narilka snapped, 'you know as well as I do that we're fast running out of suitable youngsters.'

'We'll have to send to our neighbours, see if they have any of their young men and women who would like the chance of pairing with a Portum dragon.' His voice sounded cheerful, in a forced kind of way.

Chris, realising he was eavesdropping, hurried to the door as quietly as he could and slipped out into the street. He was thoughtful as he made his way back to the dragon caves and Hess. Narilka had sounded so worried, Fallaren too, despite his cheery responses.

CHAPTER 4

That afternoon, Remnac called the whole group into their classroom. Approaching the black chalk board at the front of the room, he proceeded to write for quite a long time. Every so often the chalk squeaked causing everyone to wince.

A few of the class were reading along as Remnac wrote and before long there were dismayed gasps.

'Is this really what you expect us to do?' Ranya demanded.

'Yes,' Remnac nodded, looking very serious, 'this is what is needed from every new rider. This is what every single one of our riders has gone through. Now, it's your turn.' He stepped away from the board so they could all see what he'd written.

Daily Schedule

6am Wake, feed and bathe dragon

7.30am Bathe self, breakfast. Make bed, tidy dormitory

8.45am Lessons

12 noon feed dragons

12.30pm lunch

1pm lessons

5.30pm feed dragons

7 pm Evening meal, study, relaxation

10pm bed

'We're even told when to go to bed?' Tammy wailed. 'When do we get time for ourselves in all this?'

Silently, Remnac pointed to the word relaxation.

'That's it?' Tammy burst into tears. Ranya patted her arm awkwardly in an attempt to comfort her friend.

'What are these lessons we're to have?' asked a voice from the back of the class.

'You will study a variety of topics.' Remnac said, 'Initially the bulk of your learning will be the care of your dragons and how the bond between you works, how you can strengthen it. We will also cover basic first aid.'

'We already did that in training.' Ranya protested.

'Not like this,' Remnac said, 'in training you were told in general terms, now you are riders, you need more detail, much more.'

'Then what?' said Tammy, 'after we learn first aid and stuff, what then? Flying?'

'No.' Remnac's voice was firm, 'it will be a while before your dragons are capable of flight. Lots to do before then.'

'How long before we're assigned to a squad?'

Remnac looked for the student who had asked the question. 'It will be at least eight months, Tate,' he said to the student's obvious disappointment. 'We can't rush the process; we can't risk your dragon's health.'

Tate nodded reluctantly.

'Eight months of lessons.' Tammy wailed.

'I didn't say that.' Remnac said.

'You did! You said in eight months we'll be assigned to a squad.' Tammy was almost shouting now and many of her classmates were nodding their agreement.

'I said at least eight months,' Remnac corrected, 'and that will depend on how hard you work, you can't graduate to a squad until you've completed all your training and lessons. It will also depend on how well your dragon grows, how well you care for them. By the time they are eight months old they should be at least 70% of their adult size and capable of more prolonged flight. If they're not...' he shrugged.

'What happens if we don't pass everything? If our dragons don't grow as fast as they should?' Tammy asked quietly, seemingly determined to discover the worst possible scenario.

'You are held back until you are both ready to progress,' Remnac said simply.

Chris listened to the exchanges thoughtfully, grateful that they were all going to learn dragon care at the same time. He began to feel a little more confident of not being left behind the group. 'How do we strengthen the bond with our dragons?' he asked, thinking of the warm affection he already felt for Hess.

'There are lots of exercises we do,' Remnac said, 'we take them swimming in the lake and do trust building exercises in the water.' Chris felt less confident, 'Then there are blindfold tasks and of course the daily care of your dragon also builds on the bond you share.'

Chris nodded, 'Sounds like we're going to be fairly busy then,' he said, trying to sound light-hearted.

'Then later on you will all receive lessons in rider etiquette and public behaviour. Our riders have high standards to live up to.' Remnac said. 'You will also be taught the theory of basic fighting formations, how humans and dragons communicate with one another during an attack, what to watch out for and how to keep one another safe.'

Chris felt his head begin to reel as he realised the immense task ahead of him. He thought of the brawl at the gather the previous day and imagined what the outcome could have been if Dar's dragon had become involved and shuddered. Etiquette lessons might sound quaint, but he appreciated the necessity.

'You will also be required to make your own riding straps,' Remnac continued, 'and once your dragons are capable of flight there will be flying drills and combat instruction, putting into practice the theory I am about to teach you. And, of course, you must learn how to have your dragon flame safely. We don't want singed riders.' He gave a short laugh. 'Now, we will make a start on your education, please settle yourselves. We'll start with some basic dragon anatomy.'

The class groaned and settled themselves to study with great reluctance.

Chris, sitting alone, couldn't help wondering at the attitude of his fellow students. Surely, he thought, it was better to have a proper understanding of what was involved in the care of a dragon. He settled himself to learn all he could, determined that he and Hess wouldn't get left behind.

CHAPTER 5

Slowly, the days fell into a routine for Chris and the other new riders. Every morning they fed and bathed their rapidly growing dragons before attending to their own breakfasts and ablutions. Then came the hours of classroom lessons.

Chris was still being left strictly alone by the others in his class and every day he heard whispers following him down the corridors.

'He shouldn't have a dragon, he's too new.'

'How come he got the bronze?'

'Only been here a few weeks.'

'It's not fair, my brother missed out. Hess could have been his.'

He chose to ignore them, instead focussing his attention on Hess and strengthening their bond.

The bronze dragon was growing fast so cleaning and oiling was taking a little longer each day. Eventually, according to Remnac, he wouldn't need to be bathed so often, perhaps once a week. Chris was glad of this light at the end of the tunnel, but it was still a long way off so the hard work continued.

For his part, Hess was very fond of his companion

and very obliging when it came to bathing and oiling. Chris saw some of the other dragons squirming around and being very disobedient. He was pleased that Hess was better behaved. The pair were starting to think about flying, Hess tested his wings regularly, to the annoyance of others in the group, but his muscles were still far too weak to support flight. Chris was learning to fashion his own riding straps from strong leather, sent over by the Tannery. He wondered how Rampton would feel, sending leather over so he could make a harness for the dragon Rampton thought he shouldn't have. The making of this harness was to take up the afternoons for the next few weeks, as the apprentice riders were taught how to handle, cut and sew the leather. He was hoping that his experience of binding pages together might come in useful.

Remnac also took them through the history of Portum and their dragons. There were groans when he announced the subject, but he ignored them. Chris learned that the wild dragons were very dangerous to human habitations, that the first settlers to find Portum, exploring their new sanctuary, had stumbled upon what was referred to as the first clutch just as the eggs were beginning to crack open and, instead of destroying them as they had been instructed, they had witnessed the hatching. To avoid being attacked by the baby dragons, they had taken meat from their food pouches and fed the creatures by hand. There had only been four successful eggs in that clutch, the mother having abandoned them. The young dragons had responded to being fed by attaching themselves to those feeding them. When the men had tried to leave, the young dragons had followed them, communicating with their chosen people by sending images of fright and hunger.

And so it was that Portum became home to dragons. The leaders of the time, once they recovered from their shock at having dragons in their midst, had realised that this could be the way forward. Breeding tame dragons, which remained loyal to humans throughout their life, with which to fight back against the wild dragons.

***

When the young dragons were four weeks old Remnac announced a change to the regular classes.

'Today we will be joined by two riders,' he announced. This caused a stir and he smiled to see them sitting up a little straighter. 'They will be able to answer any questions you might have about squad structures, fighting or care of adult dragons.'

He glanced at the clock and gave a small sigh; *must they always be late?* Then the door swung open.

Every head turned to watch the riders' entrance, and Chris found himself grinning as Nat and Dar wandered in and strolled to the front of the room.

'Morning all,' Dar said.

'Alright Midget?' Nat was looking straight at Chris.

'Yeah, not bad,' he felt himself getting hot as the eyes of all the other students turned to him.

'Rem asked us to pop in today, he says you guys are full of questions about what it's really like to be a rider,' Dar continued. 'So, here we are, ask away.' He looked around the class, who returned their attention to their unexpected visitors and seemed to be having trouble gathering their thoughts.

In the lull, Chris put his hand up. 'What does it feel like the first time you fly with your squad to fight the wilds?'

'Ah, one of the big questions, Nat, you want to take this one?' Dar nudged his companion.

'Yeah, sure,' Nat perched on the corner of Remnac's desk. 'It's terrifying and exhilarating in equal measures,' she said. 'You won't fly against wilds until you're well drilled, obviously, but even so you'll feel the fear.'

'Not normal if you don't,' Dar agreed.

'How long will we be expected to train for, once we get assigned to a squad?' Ranya asked.

'All depends on you really,' Dar told her. 'If you have a good strong bond with your dragon and you both work hard, then it could be just a couple of months. If not...' he shrugged.

There were murmurs around the room at this news as the new riders realised they were facing almost a year of further training.

'What about our permanent quarters?' Ranya asked. 'Will they depend on which squad we're put in?'

'Yep,' Nat said, grinning good naturedly, 'they keep squads close to each other if they can. You'll like your space though; much bigger than the cupboards they shove you in here.' She winked at Remnac.

'What about caring for a fully grown dragon?' Tate spoke up, 'How often do they need bathing and oiling for example?'

'It depends really,' Dar told him, 'Usually, if things have been quiet, no attacks or anything, they only need to go for a swim now and again, but if they've flown against wilds, or you've been flying lots of errands, they'll need more attention.'

This sounded hopelessly vague to Chris and the rest of the class, who were hoping their dragons would become easier to look after.

'Errands?' Ranya queried.

'Yeah, you know, fetching, carrying, taking messages and so on.' Nat made it sound like this was to be expected.

'You mean they make us fly all over the place with messages?' Ranya said, sounding horrified at the thought.

'It's good practice,' Dar said firmly, 'good exercise for your dragons, helps you get used to trusting each other too.'

Ranya leaned back in her chair so hard it rocked onto two legs and she had to grab the table to stop herself falling backwards.

'Didn't they know?' Nat asked Remnac.

'I hadn't got to that part of their responsibilities yet,' he said.

'I think it sounds like fun.' Chris said. 'I spent my whole life stuck underground before Bertram and I made it to Portum, being able to fly around on Hess in the sunshine, and having a proper reason to go places, sounds great to me.'

'Yeah, well, not all of us share your enthusiasm,' Tate growled. 'I didn't become a rider to be some messenger boy, I want to fight the wilds.'

'And you probably will,' Dar said, 'but there are many parts to our work. Not only do we provide communication services to the communities we protect, but we help bring in traders and guests for gathers, if someone gets word that a relative in a different settlement is unwell, we take them to visit.'

'You need to understand, we serve our communities, not the other way round.' Nat said firmly.

'I know we're held in high regard,' Dar said, struggling to keep a straight face as he witnessed the obvious disappointment on the faces before him, 'but there's a reason for that. We protect. We serve.'

'You make it sound terrible,' Nat said, 'it's not,' she told the class, 'We have lots of fun too. And it's great doing the flying around, especially if it's been quiet, nice to get out and about.'

'We also have our work,' Dar said, still serious. 'You know, of course, that once your dragon is old enough to be left, you will be required to return to your former employment for several hours each day.'

'I thought that was optional.' Ranya tried to keep the whine out of her voice.

'No, it's not.' Dar said, his tone disapproving.

'It's one of the ways we riders integrate into the community,' Nat said, 'Besides, you'll be glad of it, believe me. Sometimes it gets a bit intense over here.'

'What if there's an attack and you're all working?' Chris asked. To his astonishment there were nods from others in the group.

'We don't all work at the same time. We have a rota to make sure there are enough of us here, just in case.' Dar told him.

Outside the room a bell sounded and Remnac stood up. 'Thank you Dar and Nat,' he said, 'I hope the class all feel this was beneficial.' There were a few nods.

'No worries,' Nat said, ever cheerful, 'If any of you have other questions and you see us around, just pop over and ask.'

'Yeah,' Dar said less certainly, 'I'm happy to answer questions.'

'Thank you,' Remnac said, 'Now class, we will have a short break.'

'See ya,' Nat said to the room in general before wandering over to Chris and ruffling his rapidly growing hair. 'How you getting on Midget? I heard this lot were giving you a bit of a hard time.'

Chris shrugged, 'Oh, I'm fine,' he said, hoping he sounded casual as the slower members of the class left the room, glancing in his direction.

Nat threw a casual arm around his shoulders, 'You'll be fine,' she said confidently, 'This only lasts for a few weeks, then you'll be out of training and over the other side with the big boys. You'll be pleased to know we're all grownups over there, well, except Dar of course.' She winked at Chris who couldn't help laughing.

Dar turned from his conversation with Remnac when he heard his name. 'Hey!' he complained, 'stop talking about me behind my back.'

'Stop turning away from me then!' Nat was on form

today and Dar gave in with a shrug.

'Let's go,' he said, grabbing Nat's arm and giving it a gentle tug. 'See you soon Chris, take care of yourself, and that little bronze monster of yours.'

Chris glanced at Remnac, who was smiling at him. 'You told them?'

'He told us nothing,' It was Dar's turn to tease, 'But you just admitted it, so now we know we have to look out once you get assigned to a squad.'

The pair of riders left. As the doors swung closed behind them, Chris heard Nat saying, 'He's a nice kid, hope he gets put with us.'

***

The following day, all the student riders had been given the afternoon off. Most of the young riders were electing to go and see their families. As Chris didn't have any family here, he was planning on staying in the dormitory and doing some reading about dragon care. The common room boasted a small library which contained scrolls and even a few books on the subject. He saw Hess settled down for his afternoon nap, then strolled out of the dormitory and along the corridor. As he walked into the common room from one direction, Jay and Anilla walked in from the other.

'Chris!' Anilla shrieked as she flew the length of the room and flung her arms about him.

'Anilla! Jay!' Chris was shocked and delighted to see his friends, 'What are you guys doing here?'

'Thought we'd come see how you're doing, over

here in dragon land,' Jay grinned, shoving Anilla aside so he could hug his friend.

'Fallaren told me you'd got the afternoon off, so we arranged to come see you. How are you settling in? Do you like the others? What's your dragon called? Can we see him?' Anilla fired off her questions rapidly.

Chris blinked and paused for a moment before answering. 'I'm settling in ok I guess,' he said, 'it's blooming hard work, looking after a dragon, you've no idea how big one is until you're required to wash it and oil it all over.' He laughed, 'his name is Hessarion, but we both like Hess. He's asleep just now, but of course you can come and see him, I was just on my way to the library.'

'You were going to spend your free afternoon reading?' Jay looked at him in disbelief.

Chris grinned sheepishly, 'Yeah, I want to make sure I know as much as I can. I missed out on the pre-training after all, I feel like I'm trying to catch up all the time.'

Anilla looked as though she were about to say something but changed her mind. 'Shall we have some batu and a catch up instead?'

'Sounds good to me.' Jay immediately made for the catering area and helped himself to a pot and three mugs. Chris followed and brought the other ingredients to make their batu the way they liked it, a jug of milk and a dish filled with soft grains of brown sugar.

Anilla chose a table and the three friends sat down. 'How are you liking it here?' she asked softly.

Chris took his time answering, pouring batu and

finishing his own to his taste. He took a sip of the steaming brew before saying, 'It's alright. It's harder work than prepping tree pulp and some of the lessons make little sense to me at the moment, but I'm sure all will become clear as we go along. And then, of course, I have Hess. No matter what I think of it here, he's worth it.' He smiled then, a radiant smile that lit his eyes and his face glowed.

Jay held his own mug in both hands, 'You know Garad and Edwin are both so proud of you, don't you?' He said, 'I'm sure they'd appreciate a visit, next time you have a free afternoon.'

Chris hadn't thought about that. 'Everyone else has gone off to see their families, but as I don't have one here, I just thought I'd be better off staying put,' he said quietly.

'Excuse me!' Anilla sounded upset, 'What are we?'

'You're my friends,' Chris replied, confused.

'So we're not worth a visit then?' she demanded.

'Well, yeah, of course you are,' Chris looked embarrassed, 'but I thought you'd both be working, so...'

'You are a rider now,' she said slowly, 'you can walk into a workplace pretty much anywhere, anytime, and ask to see whoever you please.'

'Not sure that's how it's gonna work for me,' Chris said sadly.

'What do you mean?' Jay asked.

Chris relayed to them the meeting he'd been called to and what had taken place. Both his friends looked horrified.

'They can't split a partnership like that! They just can't!' Anilla sounded worried.

'They're not going to. Fallaren held me back at the end and told me I have his and Narilka's support, which is nice. It seems they're about the only ones though.'

'Why do you say that?' Anilla asked.

'Oh, nothing,' Chris shrugged, 'just, I'm sure those masters aren't the only ones who think that way. I've heard whispers here too, they talk about me, seem to resent me being here. I tell you, if it wasn't for Hess, I'd be out of here by now.'

'If it wasn't for Hess, you wouldn't be here in the first place,' Jay pointed out.

Chris gave a laugh, 'True,' he said, 'but he's pretty much the only thing that's good here at the minute.'

'I'm sorry you feel like that,' Anilla reached across the table and touched his hand, 'this is supposed to be an exciting, happy time for you, it's sad that others are taking that away from you.'

'Oh, I'm fine,' Chris said, 'probably just tired. Ignore me. What's been happening out in the real world?'

'Well,' Jay began, 'Garad and Edwin have been approached to accept a new apprentice.'

'Have they?' Anilla said.

'Oh yes,' Jay nodded, 'Bert has been badgering anyone who will listen to let him swap from the smiths to the paper crafters.'

'Bert has?' Chris wasn't as surprised as his friends.

'Yeah,' Jay went on, 'he seems determined to move

across. Garad has said no, of course, that they already have two apprentices, but he's getting it in the neck from a few of the other masters about it. I don't think Bert's very popular in Portum, they're trying to make sure he doesn't decide he wants to join their craft halls.'

'Wow,' Chris looked stunned for a moment, 'well, I won't be unhappy if he doesn't make it into the paper crafters. I wonder what he's up to?'

'Probably wants in because of the prestige,' Jay said.

Anilla nodded, 'He does go on about it, every time I see him, he mentions his father and how important he is. I keep reminding him that he's not in Salutem now, I don't think he likes it much.'

'Probably not,' Chris said, 'he does seem full of himself since we came to Portum. Don't know what's wrong with him.'

'I think I do,' Jay said slowly, 'I think he feels he should be given rank and respect because of his position back in Salutem.'

'He was a supervisor!' Chris said, 'That's not position.'

'But his father has senior ranking, doesn't he?'

'Yeah, but..'

'There's no *but* where Bert is concerned. He thinks he's more important than he is, and he doesn't like it that no one else can see it.'

'He was one of my best mates back in Salutem,' Chris said sadly, 'we were always the ring leaders in our group. It was us who discovered the subliminal messaging. Bert was in the deep caves with us, he wasn't given preferential treatment just cos of who his dad is.'

'Are you sure?' Anilla asked.

'Yeah, he was next to me. He didn't get extra food or fewer beatings.'

His friends shuddered at the thought of such treatment. 'Beatings?' Jay asked, 'Oh man, that's bad. I know our caves weren't great, but at least they didn't set about us.'

'How long were you down in these caves for?' Anilla asked.

'A month,' Chris replied, 'we were expecting three, but they let us out, said we'd behaved so well we were being given the chance to prove we'd learned our lesson.'

'There you are then, right there.' Anilla said triumphantly, 'he may not have got preferential treatment, they couldn't be seen to let that happen, but because of him you all got out early. Don't you see? Daddy pulled some strings.'

'I never thought of that.' Chris said, sitting back and frowning, 'but yeah, I suppose you're right. Must have been a shock to him to get here and realise he was just like everyone else. Like me. Must have stung a bit.' He grinned, 'Fancy being the same as me!'

'Only he's not, is he?' Anilla said, 'because you got into the papercraft, and now you've got a dragon, and he hasn't. So you've moved ahead, in his eyes. He thinks it should have been him before you.'

'He's with a lot of other people then.' Chris said bitterly.

'No, in his case, he feels he should have got a dragon first because of his seniority over you. He was your superior in Salutem, so he should still hold that position. He's not adapting very well, is he?'

Chris thought for a moment, he could almost feel sorry for Bert, now that Anilla had spelt it out. 'I'm sure he'll be alright,' he said firmly, 'after all, there's another clutch already, isn't there.' He brightened up and drained his mug.

'There is indeed,' Jay said, grinning madly, 'and you may know a couple of people who are attending as potential riders.'

'No! Really!' Chris was delighted. He punched Jay on the arm. 'That's brilliant! I really hope you get found by a dragon, both of you, be nice to have a couple of friendly faces around here. How long till the hatching?'

'A few weeks yet,' Anilla said, 'I heard Fallaren and Narilka have been in touch with other settlements, trying to find suitable candidates for this clutch. Fresh blood you know.'

'Yeah, I heard that too,' Chris said. He told his friends about the conversation he had overheard on the morning of the meeting.

'What will happen if we run out of people?' Jay asked, rubbing his arm.

'The dragons will go wild, or die I suppose,' Anilla said sadly.

'Surely more folk will come forward though,' Chris said, 'they can't let the dragons just die!'

'I'm not so sure,' Anilla said, 'the other settlements

have dragons of their own, admittedly not as many as we have here, but they have their own communities' needs to consider.'

'If there aren't enough of our dragons, would the wilds attack us more do you think?' Jay asked.

'Yes,' Anilla sighed, 'I'm afraid that is exactly what would happen, then we're back to square one and everyone hiding in caves.'

'No!' Chris was on his feet, 'we can't let that happen. Living in caves is no life, not really.'

Jay nodded, 'I wouldn't want to go back to that, not now,' he said, 'I like the daylight and the sunshine, not too sure about the rain though.'

Anilla laughed, 'It can freak folk out the first time they experience it.' She looked at Jay who grinned sheepishly.

'Yeah,' he said, 'I ran and hid the first time it rained on me. Took Anilla ages to convince me it was safe. Poor girl was walking around outside, getting soaked to the skin.'

'I was indeed,' Anilla said as Chris laughed, 'I kept telling him 'It's only water, Jay,' but he could hardly look outside, never mind venture out to find out for himself. Narilka and Fallaren thought it was hilarious!'

'Yeah, well,' Jay coughed, 'I'm ok now though,' he said.

'You're still not keen though, are you?' Anilla said, 'I saw you last time we had rain, you did all you could to stay inside.'

Jay hung his head while Anilla and Chris laughed.

The three friends sat for a while longer, catching up with each other. Chris was very glad they'd made the effort to come and see him, it made everything seem much easier, knowing he had their friendship.

Eventually he heard soft hooting from down the corridor. 'Want to meet Hess?' he asked them.

Jay was on his feet almost before Chris had finished speaking, Anilla tidied their table before she was ready to leave. Chris led the way back down the corridor to the dormitory.

Hess raised his head as his rider approached and crooned, then he saw the other humans and suddenly he was wide awake. He hadn't encountered strangers before and he drew closer to Chris.

'It's ok Hess,' Chris said, stroking the soft neck, 'these are my friends, this is Anilla, and this is Jay, they just wanted to come and admire you.'

Hess remained uncertain but allowed them to approach him. Anilla held out her hand to him and his tongue flickered over it making her giggle. Jay repeated the action and soon Hess was confident enough to allow them to stroke him. Before long he was enjoying the attention so much he was crooning and humming, his eyes half closed. Chris couldn't help laughing at him.

Eventually Jay and Anilla tore themselves away from the young bronze, promising to come visit him again as soon as they could. Chris walked with them to the entrance to say goodbye.

'You be careful,' Anilla said as they parted, 'just remember why you're here. We're so proud of you!'

'Thanks,' Chris could feel himself flushing pink.

'See you soon mate,' Jay said, giving a final wave before they set off.

Chris made his way back to Hess and stood for a while, thoughtfully stroking his head and neck until the dragon slept once more.

CHAPTER 6

The next few days were quiet as all the new riders dealt with the day-to-day affairs of their dragons. Feeding was becoming a real chore now. The dragons were growing quickly and demanding food more often. There were complaints when Remnac informed the class that they were to be instructed in the butchery of their dragon's food.

'We don't have enough folk to be able to keep up with their demands,' he told them firmly.

A couple of the girls were very pale. 'You can't make us do that,' Ranya whined, 'I can't chop up bits of dead animal. I can't!'

'You can and you will, if you want Tathdel to thrive.' Remnac told her. 'You're all to report to the kitchen area after break.'

Chris didn't mind too much about this development in his training. 'How long until our dragons are able to catch their food for themselves?' he asked.

'At least another couple of months, possibly longer. It depends on your dragon.' Remnac told him to a chorus of groans from the rest of the group.

'Is that how long we have to wait until we learn to ride?' Tammy asked, looking forlornly at Remnac.

Remnac told them that soon the young dragons would be allowed outside to go and learn how to catch their own food. This created a flurry of excitement among the riders.

'Does that mean we're going to learn to ride?' one girl asked.

'Yeah,' a boy backed her up, ''cos they have to fly to catch food.'

'No,' Remnac said, 'they are far too young to hold your weight yet, but they must begin exercising their wings properly now, or they'll never catch anything and you'll all be lugging great buckets of meat around forever.' He grinned at their dismayed looks.

'How do we persuade them to exercise their wings?' Chris asked.

'Well, young Hess seems to be doing alright actually,' Remnac said, 'all that flapping he does is really good for his flight muscles.'

'Ah, is that what that's all about?' Chris said, 'it's a bit small in the dormitory now though, he flaps and all my books and scrolls fly across the room.' He grinned, remembering the scolding he received from some of the others at Hess's antics.

'Perfectly normal, healthy dragon behaviour,' Remnac said, 'to be encouraged by all of you,' he added pointedly. However, I take your point Chris, we'll try them outside later today if you like, start getting them used to the space.'

'Great!' Chris looked pleased. The rest of them could glower all they liked; he was the one who'd got them outside days before Remnac was going to let them. They should be thanking him.

After break, the class reluctantly followed Remnac to the kitchens where they were greeted by a surly looking man.

'This is Felix,' Remnac introduced him to the class, 'he's our master butcher and he's going to show you some basic techniques.'

Felix looked as though he'd rather be anywhere than in the kitchen with a load of raw recruits, but he nodded and hefted a heavy, long bladed knife. 'Over here,' he said roughly, turning away from his new trainees and walking to a stone table where a carcass had been laid.

He gave an informative demonstration of his skills. Ranya was almost sick and Tammy fainted and had to be carried out by Remnac and Tate. Chris, although not delighted by this turn of events, was practical enough to understand the necessity and took close note of what Felix was showing them. Hess was his responsibility after all, he reasoned, and that involved feeding him until he was able to do so for himself.

The kitchen was soon filled with the sounds of the young riders getting to grips with their food preparation, and buckets were slowly filled, ready for the next draconic meal.

'How many times do we have to do this?' Ranya asked, her nose wrinkling as she chopped at a slab of meat.

'Usually once a day at this stage,' Felix said, 'but it'll be twice a day before they're ready to go catch their own.'

'Ugh!' Ranya said, flapping her hand in an effort to dislodge a morsel of meat.

'The things they never told us about being a dragon rider.' Tate quipped.

'Yeah,' Ranya groaned, 'If I'd known, I'd have thought twice.'

'Would you though?' Chris asked, 'Isn't Tathy worth it?'

Ranya paused what she was doing, dropped her head and heaved a sigh. 'Yes,' she said eventually, 'Yes, she's worth it. She's worth anything.'

'There you are then.' Felix said, from the other side of the room, 'Stop complaining and get on with it.'

Ranya flushed bright red but bent her head to the task without further comment.

Chris smiled quietly to himself as he chopped meat for Hess.

***

After lunch, the riders led their curious dragons outside for the first time.

Sixteen young dragons and riders stood blinking in the sunlight outside the door of their dormitory. The young dragons looked around, eagerly sniffing the air and taking in their new surroundings.

Remnac appeared in front of them. 'I want you all in the correct formation,' he called. 'Most senior at the front, the rest ranged behind by colour.' He faced blank looks from the rookies and gave a sigh. 'Dragon colour denotes rank,' he continued, 'blues at the bottom of the pile, sorry,' he grinned at the groans of the new blue riders, 'then greens, you should all have seen the list. I put it up on your noticeboard last week.' When they all shook their heads, Remnac groaned. 'Right, let's do this. Chris and Hess, you will be at the front with Ranya and Tathdel.'

'Why him?'

'Because he's got a bronze, stupid.'

'That's not fair! He's not got any experience!'

'Chris, front please. Ranya, get a move on, I don't have all day,' Remnac called, 'and the rest of you, I know Chris is new here in Portum, but he's shown a capacity for work that a lot of you lack. Stop complaining.'

Chris led Hess to the place Remnac had indicated, blushing furiously and angry with himself for doing so. It wasn't his fault after all.

Remnac arranged the rest of the dragons and riders behind them. Only the silver Tathdel and her rider, Anilla's cousin, Ranya, in the front row next him. Ranya was nothing like Anilla, she seemed skittish to Chris. He had wondered many times since the hatching how she had managed to attract her beautiful dragon. He hoped her position in the ranks of new riders didn't mean he was expected to pair up with her.

'Everyone happy they know their position?' Remnac called, seeing nods and envious glances, he grinned. 'While you are still in training, this will be your squad, when you are fully trained you will be promoted to a permanent wing position with an established squad.' He saw the sighs of relief and smiled, knowing they would dislike their permanent positions just as much.

'Now, down to business,' he called, hushing the whispers which had begun at his last words, 'we are here to allow your dragons to stretch their wings without taking someone's eye out. So I suggest you spread out and then I want you to encourage your dragon to use their wing muscles. Get them flapping good and hard now, they won't be strong enough to take off, so we don't have to worry about techniques just yet.'

As he finished speaking there was a lot of shuffling as the riders encouraged their dragons away from their clutch mates. Then the flapping began, voices urged the little dragons on and soon a cloud of dust enveloped the group.

'Come on then Hess,' Chris said, 'get those wings working!' He was standing facing the dragon, crying encouragement to him.

Beside him, Ranya was giggling as Tathdel waved her wings feebly. 'She'll have to do much better than that,' Remnac said behind them, 'come on Ranya, yell at her, get her going, you don't want her falling behind, do you?' Ranya looked startled and began urging her dragon on.

Remnac was turning to walk away when Hess hooted in surprise. He had lifted from the ground, his wings working in a figure of eight motion to maintain his balance. Chris yelled and turned to find Remnac was right there with him. 'Just steady him lad,' he said to Chris, 'gentle movements Hess,' he called to the small bronze, 'slowly lower yourself back down, you know how to do it.'

Chris watched amazed, as Hess slowed his wings and gently landed again. Hess looked at Chris, his eyes whirling anxiously. Chris rushed forward to reassure him, stroking his neck and whispering, 'Well done Hess, you did it!' delightedly into his ear. Hess ruffled his wings and folded them against his back, then settled down, bringing his tail curving around his legs.

'Oh no, you're not done yet!' Remnac shouted. 'Look everyone, Hess has already taken off. Marvellous progress. Want to try again Hess?'

There was renewed energy from the rest of the squad as riders, each determined that Hess and Chris wouldn't be ahead of them, urged their dragons on to more strenuous efforts.

In front of them, Hess again flapped his wings and rose, a little unsteadily, into the air. This time he gained more height before stabilising himself. Chris didn't take his eyes off the dragon for a moment, but he was aware of the rest of his class turning to see Hess rising above them. He hung there for a few moments before gently lowering himself beside his rider. Chris was elated.

'Well done,' Remnac said, 'don't push him too much for the first day. Maybe get him flapping without lifting off. Won't be long before we take a break, don't want to overtire them, then it'll be bath time, get all this dust off them.' He gave Hess a slap on his shoulder and wandered away. Chris heard him shouting at other riders who were not as focussed as they should be.

'You heard the man,' Chris said, grinning broadly, 'flap those wings, but keep your feet firmly on the ground.' Hess huffed at him but reared back on his hind legs and flapped his wings as asked, raising a storm of dust around him. Chris coughed, holding a hand up to protect his eyes. Hess settled back down again, and Chris was sure he was looking smug. 'I think you're ready for flying lessons,' he told him, 'You're definitely ready for a bath, look at you!' Hess craned his neck round to inspect his flank. The bronze scales were no longer gleaming in the sunshine but were covered in a thick layer of dust. 'You are a very grubby dragon.' Chris told him.

He turned to look at the progress of the other dragons. Ranya had persuaded Tathdel to flap her wings in earnest now, and Tathdel, having seen how Hess did it, was sitting on her back legs flapping her wings as hard as she could. She seemed weak compared to Hess, but she was trying. Elsewhere, several dragons had given up and were crooning at their riders, only a couple of the browns were really trying.

'Right,' Remnac shouted, 'that's enough for the first day, let's get them back inside and give them all a bath. A few more sessions like this and we can get them swimming in the lake, excellent exercise for their muscles.'

Chris felt his stomach lurch at the thought, swimming was something he was hoping to avoid for as long as possible. The thought of being in deep water took his breath.

Sixteen tired dragons were urged back towards their bathing pool. As they left, Chris noticed for the first time that a lot of the older riders and their dragons had perched around the cliffs, watching this first outside exercise session. As he followed Hess towards the doorway, he heard plenty of whooping and a call of 'Well done Midget'. Grinning, he waved a hand in acknowledgement and slapped Hess on the rump as they went inside behind everyone else. Remnac closed the door behind them and they went to the bathing room.

Other dragons were already making use of the pool, so Hess had to wait his turn, sitting on his platform looking longingly at the water. One by one the other dragons were called from the water to be sanded and Hess slipped into the pool. Chris waited until the dragon was satisfied he was sufficiently wet before calling him back out to scrub him clean. All the while he was aware of curious looks and whispers from the other riders.

Finally, after all the dragons were bathed and oiled, Remnac sent them to rest.

'Lesson time,' he told the class, to a chorus of groans. 'History today,' he grinned remorselessly.

'Do we really need to know all that stuff?' Ranya whined.

'Yes! You all need to understand, fully, the responsibility you've taken on.' Remnac said, his voice stern, 'it's not all glory you know, the respect which is given to our riders is earned. The hardest work is ahead of you. Now, classroom!' He turned and left the room, not glancing back, and strode to the classroom to wait.

CHAPTER 7

A week after their first outdoor experience, Hess was capable of limited flight. Chris watched with pride, the rest of the class watched with envy, as the young bronze flew around the open space in front of the caves then, instead of coming back to Chris, he alighted on the fence of the paddock which held the herds on which the dragons fed. He sat there, flapping like a huge bird, watching the cattle with interest as they ran as far away from him as they could. His classmates were openly laughing at him when, eventually, Hess responded to Chris's commands and heaved himself back into flight and made his leisurely way back to his rider, landing neatly in front of him.

'What do you think you're doing?' Chris hissed at the dragon, 'you'll get us both into trouble!'

Remnac was bearing down on the pair, watched by the rest of the class, eager for the storm to break. 'Young Hess,' Remnac said, loud enough for the rest to hear, 'you're supposed to do one lap and come back, not go showing off.' He grinned and gave Hess a friendly slap. Behind him there were groans as it became obvious Chris wasn't going to be in trouble. 'Try and keep him controlled lad,' Remnac said more quietly, 'I know he's strong enough, and adventurous, but we need to be careful with him, don't want to lose him if there's an attack.'

As he finished speaking a shadow passed overhead and they heard the bass thunder of war cries as hundreds of dragons reacted to the presence of their enemies. In seconds dragons and riders emerged from cave openings all around the bowl. They were aloft in moments, forming their squadrons and shouting commands between ranks. Then they were off, some chasing the wild dragon which had flown across, others making sure there were no others in the area. Chris watched, delighted, as the apparent chaos resolved itself quickly into carefully ordered squads.

While the rest of the young dragons squealed and huddled next to their riders, or scurried towards the safety of the caves, Hess sat on his haunches and bellowed; his neck extended straight up. Chris was shocked at the depth of the sound coming from him. A couple of his clutch mates looked at Hess, surprise whirling in their eyes, before they were ushered back inside by Remnac. Hess took some persuading, but at last he obeyed.

'You can't fly yet,' Chris told him, 'But soon, and we'll have plenty of time to protect Portum from the wilds.' As he spoke an idea flittered across his mind, why should they always wait for the wild dragons to come to them? Why not go attack them where they roosted? He let the fleeting thought go, positive that if it were possible, Fallaren would have already tried it. Now he focussed his attention on urging Hess into his sleeping quarters.

The young dragons had grown so much that they each had a sleeping room of their own, a small version of the quarters they would have as fully grown dragons. Next to each dragon bedroom was a room for their rider. These rooms held not only beds, but also private washing and dining facilities. Chris was delighted not to have to spend so much time with his classmates. He was growing tired of being shunned by them all the time and longed for the friendly faces of Anilla and Jay. He hoped they would be joining the ranks of riders at the upcoming hatching, even though they would not be in his group at least he would have someone to go talk to in the evenings.

Once Hess was settled on his couch, grumbling but sleepy, Chris stood next to him and stroked the soft skin of his neck and head, soothing the dragon to sleep. Remnac popped his head round the curtain which gave Hess some privacy and indicated silently to Chris that he needed to speak to him once the dragon was asleep.

Chris watched as Hess slowly, reluctantly, closed his eyes and soon he heard the low rumble which was the dragon snoring. He left quietly and went to find Remnac.

He found him alone in the classroom, sitting at his desk, his head in his hands. Chris cleared his throat, not wanting to startle his teacher. Remnac looked up, his face weary.

'Ah, Chris,' he said, trying to sound like his usual self, 'come in lad.' He waved him towards a table at the front of the room and walked round his desk to join him. Once they were seated, Remnac began. 'Young Hess seems keen to get on,' he said, a little too casually.

'Yes,' Chris nodded, 'he keeps wanting to go flying farther afield, doesn't understand why he must wait for the others when they are so far behind him.'

Remnac nodded, 'I understand,' he said, 'I can remember Neldor being the same.'

'Who?' Chris asked, confused.

'Neldor, he's Fallaren's bronze,' Remnac told him, 'Sariba was like it too, she's Narilka's dragon,' he added, 'they were both ahead of the rest of their clutch too.' He looked at Chris quizzically for a moment, 'So,' he continued, 'I've had a word with Fallaren and Narilka, and they laughed. Told me I shouldn't hold you and Hess back. Fallaren,' Remnac was grinning now, 'remembered how difficult it was to control Neldor, he wouldn't want anyone else struggling like that he said.'

Chris was sitting very straight now, looking at Remnac, almost fearful of what he would say next. 'Did they say Hess and I should start flying?' he asked, his voice barely a whisper.

'Yes, yes they did,' Remnac said, 'although that will push you even further away from your classmates, I'm afraid.'

Chris shrugged, 'They already ignore me,' he said, 'I'm sure they're jealous.'

Remnac nodded, 'I know they've not been making things easy for you lad,' he said, 'and in a way I hate to pull you away like this, but young Hess won't be held back, will he?' He smiled indulgently, 'Not many young dragons are as strong as he is. I thought him being in the class would spur the others on, but it seems to be counterproductive. The others don't want their dragons to be like him, they don't want to be seen as different.' He shook his head, 'I'm going to have trouble with that lot, until they get into their permanent squads that is, then they'll knuckle down,' he chuckled, 'I've already warned the squad leaders about them, they'll find out what hard work is once they graduate.'

Chris barely heard what Remnac was saying, he and Hess were going to learn to fly! His eyes shone at the thought. 'When do we start?' he asked suddenly.

Remnac, who had been thinking about the other dragons in his care, looked surprised for a moment. 'I think tomorrow morning,' he said, 'I'll have a word with Cally, she's the instructor, see if she's available to start with you.'

Chris nodded eagerly; he could hardly keep still. He jumped up from the table, 'Want some batu?' he asked.

Remnac nodded, rising from the table, 'Yeah, you sort that lad, I'll be back in a minute.' He left the room swiftly, leaving Chris to his elation.

He poured two mugs of batu from the big jugs which were always on the table in the room's catering area and fixed his own to his liking. He put the mugs on the table they had been seated at, then proceeded to dance around the classroom, whooping joyously.

Remnac returned with a blonde woman. They stood watching Chris until he spotted them and came to a sudden stop, mid whoop. 'Sorry,' he said, looking shame faced.

'Good to see you're up for the next challenge,' the woman said to him, 'I'm Cally,' she held out her hand to Chris and he resisted the impulse to grip her forearm, instead shaking her hand in the manner he had seen since coming to Portum. He gave a small bow, he couldn't help it. Cally giggled. 'No need for that young man,' she said, 'Come, let's sit. Ah, Rem, I see you and Chris are provisioned with batu, get me one, will you?'

As Remnac sauntered over to the table, Chris sat opposite Cally. She had deep blue eyes that sparkled with mischief, he decided he liked this woman.

'Are you going to teach Hess and me to fly then?' he asked as Remnac put a mug in front of Cally and took his seat, sipping his own drink.

'Yes,' Cally nodded slowly, 'I think I am. It's early but from what I've seen and heard, I'd say young Hess is more than ready and I'd rather avoid accidents. Young dragons learning to fly by themselves can run into trouble fairly quickly, they need schooling.'

Chris was privately doubtful Hess would like this very much, but at least they would be flying. 'What's involved?' he asked, 'I haven't even finished my harness yet.'

'Why?' Remnac interrupted, 'I thought you were doing well with it.'

'I was,' Chris said, 'but some of the stitching seems to have come undone, I need to do it again.'

'Those idiots!' Remnac burst out, 'so jealous they can't see further than trying to spoil things for you, they don't see that in the end they only hurt themselves. I will be having words with them, why didn't you say something to me?'

'I...' Chris lowered his head, 'I didn't want to cause trouble, I thought if I left it, they would get bored.'

'You mean you thought if you told me, they'd get mad at you and cause more trouble.' Remnac growled.

Chris nodded and was alarmed to find tears stinging his eyes. Blinking rapidly, he covered his upset by drinking his batu.

Cally watched him carefully. 'Perhaps,' she said to Remnac, 'you might want to go have that word with the others now? I'll stay with Chris and we can discuss his new schedule and what I will expect of him and his dragon.'

Remnac gave a sigh before pushing himself up from his seat and, picking up his mug, stalked from the room. Chris heard him bellowing along the corridor for all the other riders to join him, now please. He cringed, knowing the others would be angry when they discovered he had told on them.

The issue with the harness was the latest in a long list of petty grievances, none of which he had wanted to mention before. His things were always going missing or ending up in puddles so he had no clean, dry clothing or bedding. So far, he had managed to ignore this behaviour but now he wondered if he should have done something about it sooner. He determinedly turned his attention to Cally.

'Now,' Cally had been watching him thoughtfully, she was now flicking through a book, an actual, proper book. He recognised Edwin's mark and smiled. 'What are you smiling at?' she asked.

'Your book,' he said, 'I'm apprenticed in the paper craft, I recognise the maker's mark.'

'Oh.' Cally looked surprised, 'well hopefully I can have one of your books before too long then. I do love this, so useful. Be handy if you could find a way of binding that would allow me to add pages when I need to, rather than going begging for another book. Something to think about,' she grinned at him. 'Now. Schedule.'

She spent the next half hour going through his revised schedule. He would be having fewer classes with Remnac, but his mornings would be spent outside with Cally and Hess, learning to fly, learning the tricks the dragons and riders used against the wilds during a fight. Then, of course, he would need to bathe Hess and ensure his hide was well oiled. Flying, she told him, put more stress on a dragon's hide, Hess would need more care taken of him. Bathing would also need to be done in the lake now.

'What?!' Chris was horrified. 'Why in the lake? He still fits in the pool we have indoors.' His heart was beating faster now, he'd been hoping to postpone the lake swimming lessons he knew were coming for another few weeks at least.

'Yes, in the lake,' she said firmly, 'Hess needs the extra space. Time away from his fellows, and yours, might not be a bad thing if you're having trouble with them. What's the problem?'

Chris gulped. 'I...I can't swim,' he said, 'I come from Salutem,' he continued, as she raised her eyebrows, 'No water to swim in there, and I've not been in Portum long enough to learn. I can't go in the water with Hess, I'd drown!'

'Of course you can,' Cally said briskly, 'Hess won't let you come to harm, excellent trust building exercise if you ask me. And you need to learn sooner or later, better sooner and with no audience, don't you think?'

Chris nodded miserably. From the corridor outside he could hear Remnac's voice raised angrily and the rebellious murmur from his fellow learner riders. He sighed, as if life weren't difficult enough.

The door flew open and Remnac strode in. He slammed it behind him and went to get more batu. 'I need this!' he declared, turning from the table to Cally and Chris's stunned faces. 'That lot...that lot have just told me what's been going on, and I'm sure they've not told me everything. Ranya thought it was funny!' Remnac was walking from one side of the room to the other, waving his overfull mug as he went. 'I can't believe you didn't come to me about it,' he said, slops of batu from his mug endangering Cally's book, which she swiftly moved, 'How could you let them get away with it?' He scowled and Chris cringed smaller in his chair.

'He's not cross with you,' Cally said, putting a hand on his arm. 'If I know Remnac he's cross with himself that he didn't spot what was going on and put a stop to it as soon as it started.'

Remnac nodded, 'I thought you'd all settled down,' he said, 'I noticed you didn't have many friends of course, but I didn't think there was such a campaign against you.' He shook his head and began his angry striding again.

'I didn't want to cause more trouble,' Chris said, 'back in Salutem, if you told about folk picking on you, you were the one who got into trouble.' He sighed, 'and before you say it, yes, I know I'm in Portum now, but I'm still learning how things work here.' He could feel himself beginning to tremble, 'I couldn't help that Hess wanted me, but they,' he nodded in the direction of the door, 'think I did it deliberately.'

'Yes,' sighed Remnac, 'sadly they do. I've asked them to come up with reasons why their dragons chose them, hopefully they'll see that Hess choosing you was entirely up to him.'

Chris doubted this would be a success but didn't say so. 'It's like I'm the odd one out,' he said, 'none of them like me, they won't even give me a chance.'

'Sounds like jealousy, pure and simple,' Cally said crossly, 'they ought to be ashamed of themselves, treating you that way. It's not as if you've done anything wrong, you just happened to be there and saved young Hess from, well, from dying as soon as he'd hatched if we're being honest.' She sighed and Chris saw a tear trickling down her cheek.

'I hadn't thought of it like that before,' he said, 'but once I'd paired with Hess it was like magic, I felt I could cope with anything. I'm so glad I was there so he could find me.'

Remnac nodded, 'That's the attitude lad,' he said gruffly, 'He's a good little dragon that one.'

Chris watched Cally and Remnac silently for a moment, before asking in a small voice, 'So, when do I have to start swimming lessons then?' He sounded so sorry for himself that both his instructors laughed.

'I think we'll start tomorrow morning,' Cally said, still laughing, 'while all your classmates are studying diligently with Remnac. I'm sure you can keep them all busy, can't you?'

Remnac nodded, 'Oh, they'll be busy,' he growled, 'they'll be learning exactly what it takes to be a dragon rider, and not just dragon care, it's all about character.' He grumbled on under his breath while Cally flipped through her book.

'Tomorrow morning then,' Cally said, shaking her head at Remnac, 'After breakfast, you bring Hess outside to me and we'll go through the basics and get you two airborne.'

Chris's face lit up, 'I can't wait to tell Hess,' he said.

'I don't see that holding you back will improve anything.' Cally said firmly, 'Perhaps it will do the rest of them good to see that your hard work with Hess is paying off. They can already see that you work harder than they do. Did they think that getting a dragon was the end of it? They all know they have responsibilities now, and not only to their dragon, but to themselves and to all the folk in Portum, and beyond too.'

'Chris was the only one,' Remnac said slowly, 'who hadn't had the training before the hatching, he's the only one who didn't know what to expect.'

'But he's the only one really pulling his weight, isn't he?' Cally snapped.

Remnac nodded, 'Yep, the rest of them have focussed their attention on Chris and how 'unfair' it is that he got a bronze, rather than putting their energies into learning what it really means to be a rider. They,' he said sternly, 'have a few shocks coming their way.' He slapped the now empty mug down on the table, 'I'm off to make sure they're not getting up to any mischief. See ya later Cally. Chris, try not to worry lad, you'll be fine.' With that he left the room and they could hear him shouting down the hallway at the class to be quiet.

'They'll see things differently soon,' Cally said,

'once Rem gets in this mood he'll show them no mercy. I'm sure he'll be pointing out that you didn't get the advantage of training that they've all had, and you are ahead of them purely because of your hard work.' She grinned, 'Which is about to get even harder.' She flipped her book closed and stood up, 'I'm going now, see you in the morning Chris, I'm looking forward to it.'

Chris watched her leave, wishing he could say the same. Sighing, he dragged himself up and put their mugs on the tray for cleaning before leaving the room and walking, very slowly, towards the room which held Remnac and the rest of his classmates.

As he pushed open the door every head swung to see who was coming in, and every student immediately looked away again when they saw it was him. Remnac noticed and sighed, then he gave Chris a bright smile, 'Come on in Chris, we're just running through what being a rider really is, you need to hear this just as much as everyone else.'

Chris nodded, returning the smile a little shyly, and took his usual place at the back of the room.

'Now, as I was saying,' Remnac picked up the thread of his lecture, 'being a rider isn't about fun, it's about darned hard work, relentless hard work, and bravery. Riders are courageous, they never duck their responsibilities, to their dragon or to Portum. They face attacks from wild dragons while everyone else hides, they can't sit and whine about how someone else has things better or easier than they do. Being chosen by a dragon is a hugely important event and it changes your life irrevocably, permanently.' He looked round at the faces in front of him. Some looked surprised, a couple looked stunned, only one boy at the back was nodding. Oh well, in for a penny, 'Chris, why do you think Hess chose you?'

Chris sat up very straight, shocked to have been addressed in such a way, 'Er...' he stammered as he grasped for an answer, 'I don't know,' he said, 'I was there and he was looking for me, he knew he wanted me, so I have to presume that he saw something inside of me that was special to him.'

Remnac nodded, 'Good answer,' he said, 'and you, Ranya, what do you think made Tathdel select you, out of all the available youngsters who were standing with you?'

Ranya flushed and looked at her desk, 'I'm not sure,' she said, 'perhaps she saw the funny side of me?'

'Not likely,' Remnac said, 'dragons don't think about fun in the way that we do. What else?'

'Er, well,' Ranya was obviously struggling, 'I really don't know. I don't think I'm brave, or hard working, not really. I just wanted to be a rider because I know how people here treat them, I want that respect. I guess I didn't really think about the work and stuff that's involved.'

'Even though you had the training? Twice I understand.'

Ranya blushed bright red, 'I thought they were just trying to scare us off, you know, to see if we really wanted a dragon or not.'

'Ah,' Remnac nodded, his face serious, 'and now?'

'Now,' Ranya was almost sobbing, 'now I understand just how difficult it is to look after a dragon.'

'No, you don't,' Remnac said sternly, 'you have no idea, you've only scraped the surface of dragon care.

These last weeks have been nothing compared to what's ahead of you. And now that you have your dragon, there's no turning back, you can't simply decide that you don't want to, or that you can't be bothered any more, you are a rider. You,' he pointed at Ranya, 'are Tathdel's rider. For the rest of your lives. She is not a pet, she will be a fighting dragon, and you will be with her, training her, riding her, tending her when she's injured, because she will be, they all will be.' He paused, 'But let me get this straight, there's no going back, you are chosen, not by me, I wouldn't have taken many of you, but by the dragons, and once their choice is made it's final.'

The class looked at him, more than one had tears in their eyes. 'Did you,' Remnac continued, 'any of you, really think that this training period was it? That you would be back with your families soon, enjoying the praise other riders enjoy?' There were half-hearted nods from a couple of the class. Remnac sighed, 'You, Chris, you haven't had the benefit of training and you haven't been in Portum long enough really to see how riders are treated, what was your take on being chosen by Hess?'

Chris wished Remnac would stop singling him out. Reluctantly he answered, 'I understood that once he'd chosen me, that was it, I was his and he was mine and it would be that way until one of us dies. I will look after him and, later, he will look after me. We are a pair. I once heard Fallaren say that it's an unbreakable bond that is formed.' He sighed, 'I knew, I think, in that moment, that first connection, despite the joy and excitement I felt, that my life had changed forever, but it didn't matter, because I had Hess.'

Remnac was nodding, a smile on his lips, 'And,' he

said, 'you're not afraid of hard work.'

Chris shook his head; he didn't trust himself to speak.

'Did you all hear that?' Remnac asked the rest of the group, 'Chris didn't ask for a dragon, didn't expect a dragon, but, having been chosen by one, he didn't shy away from it either. He's barely had time to get used to living outside and here he is, back in a cave,' Remnac chuckled, 'and learning how to deal with a dragon, from scratch. If he can do it, I'm sure you lot can too!' He glared around the room.

CHAPTER 8

The following morning, a nervous Chris and an excited Hess met Cally outside. She was waiting for them near the lake, which increased Chris's anxiety, but there was nothing he could do about it now. Hess was racing towards her, wings flapping.

'Hey, good morning Hess!' Cally laughed and patted Hess's neck as the dragon rubbed against her like a feline. 'Someone seems keen,' she said cheerfully as Chris joined them.

'Yes, he's been like this ever since I told him what we're going to be doing today,' Chris said, giving Hess a slap on his rump, 'He can't wait to try proper flying.'

'He might change his mind when he realises how much work is involved,' Cally said, 'now, Hess, I want you to stand straight and let Chris put your harness on you.'

Hess stood still, if not straight, and Cally handed a battered, worn harness to Chris. Under her watchful eye he attempted to put it on Hess. His fingers fumbled with the straps and he kept putting the right bit in the wrong place, but, eventually, Hess was correctly adorned.

Cally walked around the curious young dragon, checking straps, tugging at reins and seat pad, until she was satisfied all was secure and fitted correctly. 'Now,' she said to Chris, 'I want you to climb up onto the seat.' She watched for a moment as Chris jumped and struggled to get a grip before saying, 'Hess, it's usual for a dragon to extend a foreleg to assist their rider with this!' Hess immediately extended the foreleg on the opposite side to where Chris was standing, panting.

'Oh, funny!' he fumed, as Cally laughed and Hess snorted. He walked round the front of his dragon, gave him a less than friendly slap on the shoulder and proceeded to mount.

Once he had seated himself as comfortably as he could, Cally gave him instructions on how to strap himself securely into his seat and onto his dragon, along with jokey comments about how she didn't want him being tipped off when Hess turned sharply.

Chris took the advice seriously and tightened all the straps as much as he could without losing feeling in his legs.

'You're going to need this now,' Cally tossed a leather helmet to him, 'put that on and let's see if we can get you two up in the air.'

Excitement made Chris clumsy, but he managed the ties and made the helmet secure. It felt strange, but now, he was sure, he looked like a proper dragon rider. He sat and listened to Cally giving him a lecture about his posture, straightening his back when he realised it wasn't just about appearances, but also about absorbing impact on take-off and landing.

'Hess, I want you to climb onto this rock over here,' Cally indicated a huge boulder behind her. It was at least twice the height of Chris.

Chris gulped, but Hess took a confident leap. He missed the rock, landing with a bump which made Chris grateful for the straps holding him securely in place. He took a firm grip on the hand holds and leaned forward so he was almost laid on Hess, who shook his head and tried again, this time he unfurled his wings and, as he leapt, he gave a huge flap, and another, and, before Chris realised what had happened, they were sat on the rock, peering down at Cally.

'Marvellous!' Cally called up to them, 'Now come down again!'

Hess spread his wings and took a fearless jump from the boulder. Chris, clinging to the harness for dear life, could feel his muscles taking the strain of holding the wings steady as the pair glided gently to the ground. Relief flooded through Chris as he realised they'd landed safely and he hadn't fallen off. It was terrifying to him to feel so vulnerable and with so little to hold on to.

'That was really good,' Cally shouted to them, 'now Hess, if you could manage to land somewhere nearer to me that would be fabulous. Try the boulder again please.'

Chris and Hess spent the next hour practicing assisted leaps to the top of the rock and gliding down again. Landing precisely came easily to Hess, who was soon whirling around in the air to face the correct direction before coming to land close to Cally. Chris found his main job was to hang on and trust Hess.

'Your balance is coming along nicely, I think you might be ready for the next step,' Cally said at last. She turned and, placing two fingers in her mouth, gave a shrill whistle. Immediately a large blue dragon appeared in a cave mouth halfway up the cliff. He took off, gliding lazily toward his rider, circling twice before landing beside her and flipping his wings to his back. 'This show off is Finbor,' she said, giving the blue an affectionate slap, 'and together we're going to supervise your next steps in flying.'

Swiftly she mounted Finbor and fastened the flight straps. 'What we're going to do,' she called across to Chris, 'is take off and fly over the lake to the far bank. We'll land there and see how Hess is doing, then we might take a flight right over Portum.' She grinned to see how excited Chris was, 'Ready?'

The two dragons launched themselves skywards, Hess only marginally slower than the bigger dragon, and flew across the huge lake. Chris looked down and saw sunlight glittering on the edges of waves, caused by the downdraft of the dragon's wings on the surface of the lake. He felt curiously at home in the air, lack of roof and walls didn't matter now he was astride Hess's neck. As long as he remembered to keep a firm hold of the straps.

It took a matter of minutes to cross the lake. Too soon they were coming in to land, Hess manoeuvring carefully to land close to Cally and Finbor.

'How is he?' Cally asked, 'holding up alright?'

Chris checked with Hess, 'He's fine, says he wants to keep going,' Chris told her with a big grin on his face, 'this is great fun.'

'Excellent.' Cally replied, 'glad you're enjoying yourself. You need to keep an eye on him though, if you notice any signs of strain, if his colour changes or he seems tired at all, turn straight for the caves. Fin and I will follow you.'

Chris nodded, eager for the next adventure.

'Come on then,' Cally yelled, 'up we go!'

Fin leapt; Hess followed close behind. The dragons gained more height this time. Chris gulped a little when he looked down, grasping the harness and closing his eyes against the dizziness he felt. Then, slowly, they rose high enough to see beyond the cliffs right to the river, and Portum. He could feel the excitement in Hess as they began their flight. He spotted the paper crafting hut, the fishers, where someone was sitting outside mending a net, and the smoke coming from the brewers.

Then they were right over the main settlement. Buildings whizzed by beneath them, then they were out over fields again. Frightened cattle bellowed and ran as the dragons passed overhead. They were heading down the river, towards the high cliffs where it ran through the rocks. Fin and Cally began to turn, flying across the end of the huge bowl which housed Portum and coming to land at the opposite side of the river, where the grassland was wide, flat and, at the moment, free of cattle.

Hess and Chris followed suit, landing close to their teachers.

'Enjoying yourself?' Cally asked.

'Oh that was brilliant!' Chris called. Hess tried to bellow, but his voice was still developing and it came out as more of a hoot. Chris laughed and stroked the bronze neck.

'Time to go back I think,' Cally said, 'enough excitement for one morning. I think it's bath time for these two.'

Chris felt his heart sink at her words, but, he reasoned, he had to take the good with the bad, and he'd had the best morning of his life.

Hess took off after Fin, he seemed a little slower now and Chris was pleased that this was their last flight today. They flew back to the side of the lake, just in time for the rest of the class to come outside and witness them landing. Chris groaned inwardly, the last thing he needed was them witnessing him having to be taught how to swim.

He heard Remnac shouting at the class. 'One day soon that will be you, but until you put more work into your lessons and the care of your dragons you'll be stuck indoors, with me.'

Aware of the envious looks, Chris jumped down and, glancing at Cally, copied her moves and began unbuckling the straps and harness from Hess. Once all the harness had been safely removed, Fin and Hess eagerly waded into the lake, sending small waves lapping around Chris and Cally's ankles. Chris was examining the harness, it looked old and frayed, but it was still strong.

'Is this a spare or something?' he asked.

'It's an old one of Fin's,' Cally told him, 'Way too small for the great lump now though. You can use it until you have your own ready, hang onto it.'

'Thanks,' Chris folded it carefully before placing it on a rock. He was sure he could tidy it up a bit, sew in the frayed edges and oil the leather.

'Right Chris, come on, time to get these boys

scrubbed.' Cally was standing beside a large rock on which she had placed a shallow, open box of the special sand they used for the dragons. Reluctantly, Chris joined her. 'Now we have to call them to us, prepare for defiance,' Cally chuckled.

Chris called Hess, who ignored him. He tried again, the only response was Hess submerging himself and blowing bubbles. Chris glanced towards the cave entrance where the class had been standing watching, but there was no one. With a sigh of relief, Chris tried once more to persuade Hess to come out of the water to be scrubbed.

Slowly and with the greatest reluctance, Hess made his way to his rider, Fin following. The pair arrived by the rock with a big wave of water which almost knocked Chris off his feet.

'Steady!' Cally grabbed him and held him while he found his feet again. 'Now,' she said as she released him, 'you know the drill, thorough sanding, even the bits they don't like being done, then you boys can go swim to get rinsed off.' She gave Fin an affectionate slap before attacking his flank with a double handful of sand.

Chris followed suit and Hess tried to help, raising his wing to allow Chris to reach beneath the wing joint, at the same time liberally showering lake water over his rider. 'Hess! That's cold!' A bronze head looked round at his human companion, huffing hot breath at him. 'Yeah, thanks,' Chris said, batting him away, 'let me get on will you?' Hess ruffled his wings and settled down.

Chris watched Cally sanding Fin, her movements were efficient and Fin knew just how to move to allow her to get on with the job. 'How old is he?' Chris asked, panting slightly as he tried to keep pace with her.

'He's just turned three,' Cally told him, 'He's all grown up now, not that you'd know it half the time.' She grinned as Fin splashed her, 'but he's a good-natured chappie and I love him. All done now, Fin, you can go rinse off.'

Fin waddled away until he reached water deep enough for him to swim. Hess watched enviously. 'You'll get to go as soon as I've finished sanding you,' Chris told him, 'And that will be quicker if you stop your squirming,' he added as Hess wriggled while he tried to sand under his belly.

After a few more minutes he gave Hess a thump on his shoulder, 'go on then, off you go.' Chris watched as Hess lumbered after Fin, eager for another swim with his new friend.

'Now all we've got to do is get you in there with them,' Cally said, right beside him now.

'Well, I mean, I don't really need to go right in, do I?' Chris said, 'I mean, look at them, they don't need me at all.'

'You need to learn how to swim,' Cally said firmly, 'just in case.' She gave a shrill whistle and Fin obediently swam towards her. Cally took a firm grip on Chris's arm and marched him out into the lake. 'Now, you grab Fin's neck ridge here, like this,' she demonstrated, 'and hold on tight.' Chris did as she said and Fin took off for the centre of the lake again, swimming far too quickly for Chris's liking.

Hess looked round in surprise and greeted his rider with a hoot, swimming towards him playfully. Behind him, Chris heard a regular splashing. He looked over his shoulder and saw Cally swimming towards him with firm, regular strokes.

'Let go of Fin now,' she said as she caught up with him, 'and let yourself relax, you'll be fine, I promise.'

Chris doubted that very much, and kept a firm grip on Fin's neck, but the blue dragon began to dive and he was forced to let go. At first he floundered, splashing and going under the water.

'Stop panicking,' Cally yelled, grabbing his shoulder and pulling him to the surface, 'Now, move your legs in circles and wave your arms like this on the top of the water and keep your head up.' She demonstrated and Chris tried his best to copy her moves. After a couple of minutes of spluttering, he finally got the hang of it. 'This is called treading water,' Cally told him, 'And it's the most basic way of keeping afloat.'

Chris turned in a circle, gradually feeling more confident, until a thought struck him. 'How do I get out?' he asked.

'Hess will take you this time, but we'll have proper swimming practice every day from now on. We need to get you confident in the water before that lot,' she jerked a thumb in the general direction of the caves, 'get out here with their dragons.'

Chris agreed wholeheartedly with that idea and promised himself he would work hard, despite his fear of the water. Hess surfaced next to him and he grabbed his neck and pulled himself astride his shoulders.

Following Fin, Hess swam steadily back to the shore and waddled out of the lake. Chris slipped down and grabbed up the harness. Hess, he noticed, was drooping slightly and his colour had become a dull brown rather than his usual glistening bronze.

'We need to get you back to barracks,' Chris said in a purposely cheerful tone, 'Time for a nap.'

Cally looked over and nodded, 'Yes, let him have a good old shake to get dry, then it's definitely nap time.' She grinned at Chris, 'you did well today, both of you. Same time tomorrow morning.' With that, she leapt onto Fin's back and, with a great heave of his wings, Fin took them back to their living quarters.

'You heard her,' Chris said, giving Hess a nudge, 'let's get you to bed, you look tired.'

Hess followed his rider, he was tired but he was very happy with himself, he kept nudging Chris in the back and making little humming noises. By the time they got to their sleeping quarters though he was drooping. He climbed onto his bed platform, curled up and, blinking sleepily, looked up at Chris, who stood close to him and gently stroked his neck and head until he heard the gentle rumble which signalled a sleeping dragon.

CHAPTER 9

That afternoon Remnac informed the class that there was to be a Gather at the end of the week. As the class whooped their excitement he held up a hand.

'Some of you will need to stay here,' he said, to a chorus of groans, 'it will depend on your dragon I'm afraid. Some of them are still too immature to be left,' he looked around the class and fixed his gaze firmly on Ranya.

'You mean, I can't go to the Gather with everyone else, and see my family and friends?' Ranya had tears in her eyes.

'I'm afraid not,' he said, 'Tathdel isn't ready for you to be away for a full day, not to mention she would feel the excitement you feel and it would unsettle her too much. The same, sadly, goes for a few of you. This isn't the same as an afternoon off to go see your families, this is a Gather, with all the noise and excitement that goes with it, and young dragons often struggle to cope.' He waved a piece of parchment at them, 'this is a list of those who must stay put, and those who can choose to go to the Gather if they wish. I'll put it on the noticeboard later. Any questions?' He looked around the classroom at the subdued faces and sighed, it was always like this the first time. 'You will be able to go to Gathers again,' he said, 'just not this one, your dragon must come first. Now, lessons.' He strode to the desk and began the afternoon's lecture on safety procedures.

Once the class was finished, Remnac stuck the parchment on the board as promised and left the room. Everyone made a dash for the board, crowding round pushing and shoving, trying to see the list. The list of those able to attend the Gather was short. This elicited much complaining which, Chris thought, was probably why Remnac had disappeared as quickly as he had. He waited until the crowd around the board had thinned and people had started to leave the room before he strolled over. He saw his own name on the list and smiled. It would be nice to have the chance to catch up with Anilla and Jay and see how their training was going.

'What are you smirking at?' said a female voice.

He turned to see Ranya glaring at him. 'I'm not smirking,' he said quietly, 'I'm just pleased I get a chance to go see my friends.'

'Lucky for some,' she snarled, 'you and your precious bronze get to do everything before the rest of us, don't you?'

Chris frowned, 'I suppose,' he said slowly, 'but Hess and I work hard. I don't want to be stuck in this classroom for ever, so I make the effort to learn what I need to know, and I work hard at looking after Hess so we can be free of Remnac and his lessons.'

'Oh.' Ranya looked stunned. 'I hadn't thought of that,' she said.

'No, I know you hadn't,' Chris said with a sigh, 'You're all too busy being cross with me for having a dragon. I didn't choose this, but you all did and I really can't understand why you would mess about rather than getting stuck in and becoming proper riders.'

Ranya's face, blotchy from her crying, paled as he spoke and her eyes shifted to the door behind him.

'That is exactly what I've been telling them,' Remnac said behind Chris, 'It's all down to them and how well they study, how hard they work with their dragons. It's not just a case of sitting in a classroom until the dragons grow enough to fly and then lording it over the rest of Portum. It's responsibility and hard work, and lots of it, that make a rider, along with bravery and observational skills most of your class don't seem to possess.'

Ranya gulped, grabbed her things and dashed out of the room. Chris could hear her sobbing as she ran down the corridor.

'Well done lad,' Remnac said, 'I hope she tells the others what you just said. I've been trying to drill it into their skulls all morning. You should have heard them moaning about how unfair it was that you and Hess got to go flying. I told them, you do the work, you can go flying too. Didn't go down too well,' he grinned and shrugged, 'They'll learn eventually, they all do. Dragons first.'

Chris nodded, 'Speaking of which, I'd better go and check on Hess, he was a funny colour after our adventure this morning.' He turned and was almost out of the door when Remnac spoke.

'He'll do well, that little bronze of yours. He's brave, bit headstrong, but you'll control that I'm sure, and he's eager to learn, like his rider. The two of you will do very well. Cream always rises.'

Chris gave him a puzzled look but thanked him and hurried off to see Hess.

The sleeping room was quiet, except for the deep rumble of Hess snoring. Chris stood and looked at him, his hide now gleaming bronze again. He couldn't hide his pride or pleasure in his dragon, he forgot the hard work and the boring lessons as soon as he was with Hess. A cough made him turn around. Several of his classmates were standing outside in the corridor, Ranya among them.

'Can we have a chat?' she asked him.

Chris nodded a little uncertainly. 'Common room?' he asked.

'Please.' Ranya's voice broke as she spoke and she turned and hurried away followed by the rest of the group.

Chris stood for a minute, attempting to gather his thoughts before he wandered down the corridor and into the huge common room. A group of six or seven of his classmates were waiting for him.

Ranya stood as he entered the room and gave him a shy smile, waving him to join them. 'Thanks for coming Chris,' she said, the rest of the group murmured greetings and nodded at him.

'What's going on?' Chris asked, noting several of the group had red eyes and noses, he presumed there had been lots of tears.

'Well,' Ranya began uncertainly, 'I, that is we, wanted to say how sorry we are for the way we've treated you.' She seemed to deflate as she spoke and flopped down into one of the upholstered chairs before continuing. 'I think we thought that being a rider would be fun, an adventure, but it's hard!' Her voice was almost a wail as she finished.

'But you had the training,' Chris said, puzzled, 'Didn't they tell you how much hard work is involved in looking after a dragon and learning all that you need to know about becoming a rider?'

Ranya and a couple of the others nodded miserably. 'I didn't believe them,' Ranya said.

'You saw the glamourous side and thought that was all there was to it?' Chris guessed.

There were nods from several people, they all looked unhappy.

Chris shook his head, 'I know I didn't have time to get the training,' he said, 'but even I understood that there would be an enormous amount of work involved.' He took a seat and leant forwards, his elbows on his knees. 'And then you all got so tied up being angry at me for getting Hess, I've no idea why, and seemed to forget why we're all here.'

Ranya sniffled, 'I wanted everyone to treat me the way the other riders get treated,' she said, 'I'm the youngest of seven and no one's ever thought I was special before, getting a dragon made me different, my parents noticed me for the first time in months…years…and I fell in love with my Tathy, I just didn't realise how much work there would be.'

'And the lessons,' groaned Tammy. She and Ranya were good friends as far as Chris could make out, they were usually together. Several groans from the others showed their agreement with her gripe.

'But,' Chris said, 'you knew all this before you attended the hatching, didn't you?'

Ranya and Tammy nodded; Tammy blew her nose noisily. 'They told us all about how to look after our dragons for the first few days,' Ranya said, 'but it didn't sound too bad. Bathing them was like bathing a baby really, and I thought they would be able to feed themselves and stuff really quickly, but it's been weeks!' Her voice was a thin wail, 'And now we can't even try flying yet because Remnac says we're not good enough.' Tears were trailing down her cheeks now and she fumbled for her handkerchief.

'Yeah,' Tammy sniffed, 'we thought we'd all be flying by now, cos it's what dragons do, isn't it? They all fly and we just have to get on and not fall off.' She gave a weak smile and someone else gave a half laugh, 'But it looks like we still have loads of work to do,' she continued, 'and even when we're flying there's work to do. When do we get time for ourselves? I mean, we need to get back to work, we need to be able to go see Jen and get our hair cut and...' her voice trailed off when she saw the look on Chris's face.

'You're bothered about getting your hair cut?' he said incredulously, 'being a rider isn't about a haircut, it's about protecting Portum, about being of service to the community.' He stopped, unable to believe that these girls could be so naïve.

'I know we're all taught to honour the riders,' Ranya said quietly, 'but I suppose I never thought about what they have to do every day.'

'You thought you'd get a dragon, look after it for a couple of weeks, and then go back to normal?' Chris said scornfully, 'You thought a baby dragon wouldn't need months of care to get to fighting size and strength? You thought you wouldn't need training to know how to fight on a fire breathing dragon? You thought you could just sit there looking pretty? Is that what you've seen others doing? Or have they been up there, braving the attacks to save your skin?' Chris was on his feet now, his face flushed with anger. He took a few deep breaths, noting the look of horror on the faces around him. 'What, exactly, is it you want from me?' He asked, looking round the group.

'We hoped you might be able to forgive us for being so nasty to you,' Ranya said, 'and that you may be able to help us with the lessons, I find them so difficult, and so dull.'

Chris thought for a moment and took a couple of deep breaths, how things changed. 'I think,' he said slowly, 'that I will accept your apology, so long as there's no more bullying, but I really don't know how I can help you with your lessons. I'm in the same state you are, I just decided that I need to learn what Remnac's trying to teach us, so I better pay attention, even though I find it difficult.'

'Could we meet up in the evenings, do you think, and maybe go over the stuff he's talked about that day, so we all understand it?' Tammy was still pale but there was a glimmer of a smile on her face now.

'I don't see why not,' Chris said.

'And maybe you could tell us about flying too,' Ranya said breathlessly, 'Is it difficult?'

Chris hid a grin, 'It's complicated,' he said, 'there's more to it than I thought, and Hess tired fast. I have a feeling it'll be a long process.' He grinned at the groans this comment elicited.

'So even when we're allowed outside, we still have to work hard?' Ranya didn't seem impressed.

'Yes, and then it's lesson in the afternoons, after you've seen to your dragons, naturally.' Chris was starting to enjoy this.

A bell started ringing and the bowl outside was suddenly filled with the sounds of running feet and shouting. The trainees looked at each other before running out of the room and to the huge doors which led to the outside. Not for the first time Chris noted the similarities to the great doors which kept the population of Salutem contained.

They stood on the threshold, looking at the scene as riders and dragons scrambled, just as the first wild dragon appeared above the cliffs. Within seconds all the fighters had taken off and the air above the cliffs was filled with roars and the smell of phosphorous as the dragons flamed.

A huge, black dragon appeared, so low Chris could see his belly scales and the tip of his tail almost touched the top of the cliffs opposite. His eyes glowed when he spotted the group of youngsters watching and he began to dive, roaring and preparing to flame at them. They darted back inside and banged the door shut as they heard more roars and shouting. The Portum dragons were attacking the interloper. There were screeches of pain and the smell of burning flesh penetrated the doors as Chris and the rest of the group cowered in the corridor.

He was dying to open the door a little and have a look at what was happening but thought better of it. Safety of the group was more important than his curiosity. What would Hess do if he got injured, or worse? He could hear the hoots and rumbles of the young dragons as they reacted to the noise outside.

Remnac came running down the corridor to the group, his relief at their safety obvious. 'Go to the common room,' he ordered, before picking up the heavy timbers which were used to bar the great doors and fitting them into the slots which held them. He'd often told the class that this made the doors so strong even a dragon couldn't break them down. None of them had wondered why this was necessary, until now.

As the class made their way to the common room the noises outside faded away. The room was silent until Remnac arrived. He looked shaken but determined.

'What just happened?' Tammy asked, raising her hand.

Remnac gave a heavy sigh and sat down on the nearest chair. 'That,' he said, 'was the worst attack, and the closest call, we've had in many years. That black dragon seems to have become the leader of the wilds and he's a nasty one. I can't believe he was targeting you.'

'What was that smell?' Ranya asked him, her nose wrinkled.

'That, was dragon flesh being burnt, by the fire of another dragon.' Remnac said sadly.

'Oh!' Ranya's eyes were round and scared.

'Was it one of ours?' Chris asked.

Remnac paused before nodding, 'Not just ours though,' he said, 'We got him good and proper, not sure how he was still able to fly if I'm honest, one of his wings was badly injured, and he'd been flamed all down one side.'

'Is there anything we can do to help?' Chris asked.

'No lad, but thank you.' Remnac's smile was tired and he looked worried. 'I have to go see to the injured. I'm glad you're all safe. Go make sure your dragons are alright, they'll be frightened, as the fighting was so close to them.' He heaved himself to his feet and left.

Chris didn't wait to see what the others were going to do, he left the room at a trot and headed straight for Hess, who he found sitting upright in his bed, neck outstretched hooting. He ran to the dragon and began soothing him, smoothing the long neck, stroking his shoulders and gently folding his wings back against his sides. He murmured all the while, telling Hess it was all ok, that they were safe and that one day soon he would get to fly against the attackers. They would repay the bravery which had been shown today in defending them.

CHAPTER 10

A few days later, Chris was heading out with Hess to meet Cally when he heard his name called. Turning, he saw Seb trotting across the huge inner bowl.

'Hey!' Seb said, rather breathlessly, 'how are you?'

'I'm great, thanks Seb, good to see you.' Chris replied, 'what are you doing here?' As he spoke he guessed the answer.

'I've been sent to help out the healers,' Seb told him, 'There were quite a few injuries the other day and one of the riders is in a bad way. I am the official support.' He tried to grin but didn't quite manage to take the worry out of his eyes.

'Good luck,' Chris said, 'I didn't know about the injuries, they don't tell us much, probably don't want to scare us.'

Seb nodded, 'More than likely,' he said, 'better get going, see you later perhaps?'

Chris nodded and stood for a moment, watching his friend scurrying across to the huge caves which housed the medical facilities for dragons and riders alike. Turning, he jogged to catch up with Hess, who was already standing near Cally and Fin, ready for his flying lesson.

'You ok?' Cally called as he got near to her.

'Yeah,' he panted, 'Just saying hello to a friend of mine, he's been sent over to assist our healers. He says one of our riders is in a bad way?'

A shadow passed across Cally's face, 'Sadly, he's right,' she said quietly, 'That black dragon is a brute. We got him, but he seared a couple of dragons and, as your friend said, one of our riders is badly burnt. His dragon is injured too, and worried about his rider, so the healers are having to deal with both of them.'

'Will they... I mean, do you think they'll be alright?' Chris asked.

Cally shrugged, 'I hope so, we all do, naturally, but I'm afraid this is all part of being a rider. We all take risks to save the rest of Portum.'

'Attacks like this are the reason people fled to the caves, aren't they?'

'Yes, sadly attacks were frequent back then, and we hadn't learned how to protect ourselves. Can't really blame folks for running and hiding.'

Chris shook his head sadly. He stood for a moment lost in his thoughts until Hess nudged him gently with his nose and Chris looked up into those rainbow eyes and smiled, how could he feel sad when he had Hess? 'One day,' he whispered, 'one day we'll be up there, it'll be our turn.'

'Not unless you get this training done,' Cally said briskly. She was fastening the last straps on Fin's harness.

Chris moved swiftly to fasten Hess's harness and, with the help of a thoughtfully extended foreleg, he clambered to his seat at the base of the neck. He took hold of the straps as he'd been taught and looked expectantly at Cally, who was still standing next to Fin.

'Off you go then,' she called, 'other side of the lake. Land and wait for instructions.'

Chris gave Hess the order and the pair were off. Two great heaves of Hess's wings and they were airborne and gliding over the lake. Chris had forgotten his initial fear now, this was his favourite thing, his favourite place to be. The wind rushed past his face, battering his ears. He wondered why the helmets riders wore didn't provide protection for the ears and made up his mind to ask Cally when they got back to her.

Hess landed neatly and the pair looked back across the lake for their trainer, but Cally and Fin were nowhere to be seen.

'Where've they got to?' Chris wondered aloud. Hess rumbled his concern. 'Should we go back over?' Chris said thoughtfully, but Hess reminded him that Cally had said to land and wait for instructions. So they waited.

They sat there for a full three minutes, scanning the opposite bank of the lake when suddenly Fin and Cally were there with them, behind them. Cally laughing at the astonishment on Chris's face. Hess hooted in surprise and turned round to face Fin.

'Where did you go?' Chris demanded, 'how did you do that?'

Cally signalled for him to dismount, then slid down Fin's foreleg to join her student on the sand.

'That,' she told him, 'Is what we call blinking.' She

smiled at Chris's confusion.

'But blinking is what you do with your eyes,' he said, demonstrating.

'It's also something that some riders and dragons can do,' she told him, 'Not everyone manages it, and we've had some terrible accidents over the years, so we don't advertise the ability now, we just look out for likely candidates to teach.'

'And you think Hess and I could do it?' Chris breathed excitedly.

'Perhaps,' Cally conceded, 'Remnac seems to think so. Hess is very agile and he picks things up fast. Only trouble I can see is that you're both apt to rush into things, and we can't afford to lose you, either of you.' She looked up at Hess, who had swivelled his head around to watch what was going on. His eyes swirled innocently at her and she laughed, 'You don't fool me, you great bronze lump!' Hess hooted at her. The hoot turned into a rather deep growl and the young dragon sat back on his haunches looking surprised.

'What was that?' Chris wanted to know.

'His voice is breaking,' Cally laughed, 'Just like yours did. Dragons go through the same process.'

Hess tried again, but his usual high-pitched hoot came out.

'It won't be long before he's found his adult voice,' Cally told Chris, 'Then you'll know you've got him, I reckon he'll have a lovely deep voice, and they do love to bellow when they find that they can.'

'Something to look forward to,' Chris said wryly.

'Now, what's this about blinking?'

'It's a complicated little trick some of the dragons can master,' she said, 'it requires excellent communication between rider and dragon, and it's not something to be taken lightly, as I said, accidents happen and they're nasty.'

'Hess and I communicate well,' Chris said eagerly.

'I know,' Cally gave a grin, 'but I admit I'm not quite as sure you're ready as Rem seems to be. So, I thought that this morning you could try some of the preparatory exercises if you like. We'll keep the session short because Hess will tire more quickly, and then he can have a nice bathe while you get your swimming lesson.'

Chris felt his stomach churn when she said it. Since the first session when he'd learned to tread water Cally had made him go in the water every day, teaching him basic swimming strokes. He still wasn't comfortable in the water but at least he knew how not to drown. He faced it every day, like an approaching moment of doom after an exciting morning learning new skills. He sighed. 'Ok. What do you want us to do?'

They spent the next hour demonstrating to Cally that they had good communications skills, that Hess would listen to his rider – although this took longer than Chris had hoped – and that they knew the area around the lake incredibly well. Cally wanted far greater detail than Chris had expected and he and Hess had to fly around several times, noting tiny things he'd never seen before, patterns in the pebbles, the exact shape of a rock. His brain was aching by the time she signalled them to come in to land next to her.

'I want you to recreate what you've just seen,' Cally said as he dismounted. She'd smoothed an area of sand and handed him a short stick. Chris, tongue stuck out in concentration, did his best to draw the far shore, paying particular attention to the big rock with the weirdly shaped crack that Cally had mentioned several times. His attempts were hampered by Hess, who insisted on looking over his shoulder and commenting on his efforts, pointing out bits he'd missed and once huffing so much he erased part of the sketch.

Finally, Chris was happy the drawing was complete and he stood up, looking over to Cally for approval.

'Hmm, not bad,' she said slowly, 'you missed the pebbles though.'

Chris could have kicked himself, especially when Hess reminded him, rather tartly, that he'd said about the pebbles.

'Won't the pebbles shift over time?' he asked, attempting to deflect her from any other shortfalls.

'Nope, they've been fixed in place specifically for this purpose,' she told him, 'No one really notices them until we teach this technique. But those pebbles in that pattern are one thing that will always allow you to get home.'

Chris nodded but he still didn't really understand. He was tired, Hess was being snarky, and he still had the swimming lesson in the lake looming over him. He flopped to the sand, drew his knees up and rested his chin on them with a heavy sigh. 'What's all this about anyway?' he asked.

'You need to recognise these points,' Cally pointed

to the sketch, 'and many others too, in different places around Portum, and farther afield, in order to use blinking. It allows your dragon to transport you, more or less instantly, to wherever you need to go.'

Chris sat up, eyes wide. 'You mean like time travel?' he breathed.

'No, not like time travel,' Cally said, 'we don't travel to a different time, just a different place. And it's dangerous, very dangerous.' She sounded stern so Chris did his best to look serious, although the gleam in his eyes gave away his excitement.

'When do we start?' Chris asked, forgetting how tired he'd felt a moment before.

'Tomorrow. Perhaps.' Cally said thoughtfully, 'There's no rush, and you don't want to start this when you and your dragon are already tired. The training is hard, and you two are still green.' She shook her head, 'I'll see what Rem says later, but I remain unconvinced.' She looked at him then gave a sudden grin. 'Hess, bath time!'

Hess brightened up immediately, Chris groaned.

Cally swung up into her seat on Fin, 'Come on,' she said, 'let's get over to the other side and get these boys into the water.' Fin heaved his wings and leapt skywards.

Hess fussed and hooted while Chris got himself organised. After a moment's hesitation he scrubbed his sketch away with his boot, then he clambered up onto Hess and gave the command to lift off. Hess leapt as Fin had done and seconds later they were gliding over the lake. Usually this exhilarated Chris, but he could see Cally already preparing to go in the lake. Fin was already up to his shoulders in the water, rolling lazily and causing waves to reach his rider.

Chris and Hess landed, and the little bronze could hardly keep still long enough for Chris to remove the harness. He half flew, half trundled into the lake to join his friend, hooting happily. Chris looked at Cally, who was kitted out in shorts and a rather tattered looking top. She was waving a similar outfit at him.

'Come on,' she called, 'let's get you changed into something less likely to drag you down,' she indicated his leather flying gear, 'and then you can have a serious swimming lesson!'

Chris obeyed reluctantly and was soon standing waist deep in the lake feeling very nervous. Cally handed him a board. He took it, mystified. It was lighter than it looked, and he tossed it from one hand to the other.

'What's this for?'

'This is what we call a float,' Cally told him, 'And it's going to help you not drown, or rather, it'll help keep you up while you learn the fine art of swimming. It's time to finesse your technique a little.'

Chris got the feeling she was enjoying this a little too much, he made up his mind to learn how to swim properly as quickly as possible, if only to stop her gloating. He listened carefully to her instructions, then crouched down in the water, shivering as it closed over his shoulders. Then, holding the board out in front of him with both hands, he lifted first one foot, then the other and kicked with all his might.

There was a lot of splashing and not much movement, but the board kept his head above water. Behind him he heard Cally coughing and realised his splashing had caught her. Putting his feet down again he turned to look at her. She was wet through, water streaming from her hair, she wiped her eyes and laughed.

'Ok, that was...enthusiastic.'

Chris grinned unrepentantly, 'Well, you did say to kick as hard as I could.'

'So I did. Come on then, try again.'

This time she moved out of the way of his ferocious kicking and gave him advice on how to keep his feet in the water.

Slowly Chris began to move forwards, Cally swimming alongside. He stopped and tried to put his feet down, realised he couldn't feel the bottom and began to panic. Cally was next to him, grabbing his arm.

'Don't panic, keep hold of your board with one hand and move your legs and arms so you tread water. Remember? I'm here, you're ok.'

Chris tried to remember how it had felt to tread water and, spluttering from swallowing what felt like half the lake, he began to move his legs in circles. Hess surfaced next to him, eyes gleaming. He hooted playfully then swam off, giving his tail a flick which splashed water at his rider.

Chris spent the next half hour splashing around in the lake, slowly refining his leg movements so he could move forwards rather than creating splashes. Cally indicated he should head for the shore and he did so, turning easily in the water now.

'Good work,' Cally said as he stumbled out of the water, 'tomorrow we'll try without the board.'

Chris shook himself like a dog and reached for the drying cloth she'd laid on the big rock for him. Although her words filled him with dread he gave a shrug, 'OK,' he said, hoping his voice didn't wobble too much, 'I've got to learn.'

Cally nodded in approval, he was brave this one, and, as Remnac had said, a hard worker.

They called the dragons to them and began the business of sanding them clean. Chris was exhausted by the time he sent Hess out into deeper water to rinse himself. Eventually, dripping wet, with a damp towel around his shoulders, he made his way to their living quarters, Hess waddled along behind complaining he was hungry.

'Hungry? You only ate a few hours ago!' He could hear Cally chuckling and in his mind he heard her chanting about growing dragons needing food and rest. 'Come on then, you've worked hard this morning, let's see if I can scare you up some lunch.' Hess waddled faster and beat Chris to their quarters.

Chris, still dripping lake water, went in search of a bucket of meat for the dragon and returned a few minutes later, to find Hess curled up in his bed, fast asleep. He waved a piece of meat directly under his nose, but there wasn't so much as a twitch. With a sigh he covered the bucket with a cloth and went to find some clean clothing.

Dry and dressed, he sauntered down to the common room and helped himself to some batu. Down the corridor he could hear the rest of the class turning out of the classroom and heading in his direction. He took a seat and put his arms on the table, leaning forward with a sigh.

Ranya was first in, complaining loudly about Remnac's class. She stopped short when she saw Chris. 'Are you alright?' she asked, approaching the table Chris was sitting at. She touched his shoulder and Chris looked up wearily at her. 'Oh my! What happened?'

'Flying. Swimming. Bathing and feeding. The usual.'

'At least you get outside to fly!' Tanya sounded angry and there were several murmurs of agreement from the rest of the class. 'All we want to do is learn to fly, on animals which are made for it. How hard can it be?'

'Very.' Chris said quietly.

His quiet response got the attention of everyone. There was a loud shushing and calls for silence and gradually all chatter ceased. Mugs of batu were handed round and his classmates drew up chairs from other tables to sit around Chris, who sat, a reluctant guru, in the middle.

'What's it like?' It was Ranya asking, her voice was softer now, she almost sounded concerned for him.

Chris looked up at her, 'That noise we heard the other day, that smell? I saw my friend as I left barracks this morning, he's a healer, been sent for to help out with the injured. That big black dragon got a couple of ours, and one of our riders is in a really bad way. The smell was dragon, burning dragon.' He looked sadly into his batu for a moment as they all absorbed what he was saying. 'One day soon, that could be us.'

'And the flying?' Tanya asked, pushing aside the

thoughts of what flames could do to her and her dainty little green dragon.

'Is hard work,' Chris said, 'there's a lot more to it than sitting on a dragon and having it fly wherever you want to go.' He took a swig of his batu and then told them about his gruelling schedule, about how physically demanding flight was, and when that was over the drills and the bathing, which was no longer fun as there was a lot more dragon to scrub. 'And of course, after all that, it's more lessons with Remnac,' Chris finished with a heavy sigh and drained his mug.

The room was silent for a moment, then everyone started talking at once. The main complaint seemed to be that there would be no release from the classroom. Chris lowered his head to his arms to hide his grin.

Remnac walked in and called for quiet. 'What's all this noise about?' he demanded, waving the group into silence when everyone tried to tell him at once. 'You.' He pointed at Tammy, 'what's going on?'

'He says we still have to do classes, even when we're outside learning to fly.' Her voice had taken on an unpleasant whine.

'Not at the same time,' Remnac smiled, 'but yes, you are unlikely to have completed your classes by the time your dragons are ready for flight. You've all seen Chris in the classroom in the afternoons, you already know this.' Groans met this statement. 'You'd rather I hold your dragons back until you're done with classroom learning?' Remnac asked them.

'No! We didn't say that!' A tall boy named Tomas said, he sounded panicky, 'We were just surprised, that's all.'

'Well, if you all worked a little harder in class, you'd be able to graduate sooner.' Remnac said quietly, before turning and walking over to the table to help himself to batu. He poured two mugs and took one over to Chris, putting it down in front of him. 'You look worn out,' he said, just loud enough for the others to hear.

Chris raised a weary looking face and gave a half smile to his teacher. 'Yeah, this morning was tough,' he said, 'it's not just the flying, it's all the technical stuff I've got to learn too. Makes my brain hurt.' He gave a sigh before reaching for the second mug of batu.

'Technical stuff?' Tammy sounded concerned.

'Yeah, it's all about angles and...stuff.' Chris trailed off, not wanting to mention his extra training with Cally in the art of blinking. He supposed not everyone would be offered that and he didn't want to break his fragile rapport with the group.

'Angles?' Tammy looked confused.

'Yeah,' Chris said, 'it all got a bit weird today, I guess cos we've got to know where we're going when we're flying, it was all about recognising places from different viewpoints, even though I haven't been there yet. The actual flying is hard on the dragons too, they can only take so much before they tire.'

Silence met his comments and Chris, not daring to look at Remnac, drank his batu then, with obvious reluctance, pushed himself to his feet. 'I need to eat,' he announced, strolling towards the tables at the end of the room, which was now laden with covered dishes. He took the covers off, allowing the aromas to spread around the room. Shortly he was joined by several other class members as he piled his plate with potatoes and vegetables. He added meat and gravy, grabbed some bread, and went back to his seat.

Remnac was still sitting at the table. 'Hungry?' he asked, raising an eyebrow at the amount of food on Chris's plate.

'Starving!' Chris mumbled through a mouthful of potatoes. He swallowed and grinned. 'Cally's a slave driver.'

Remnac nodded, 'I know it's hard work,' he said.

Chris shrugged, 'They'll all find out soon enough,' he said, 'at least now they've got some idea of what's to come.'

Remnac nodded and gave Chris an odd little smile before leaving the table to go and get his own meal.

The afternoon's classes dragged. Chris was sitting at a table with Ranya, Tammy and Tomas. They had been tasked with drawing a plan of the Portum area, from the point the river emerged from beneath the rocks, across to the fishers and the paper crafters, which gave Chris a pang - he missed his job - right up to the dragon caves and the lake. They were arguing about the size of the farms at the moment and Chris sighed.

'Look,' he said, patience straining his face, 'If we put the main settlement in, and the river, then everything else can be slotted in around those, can't they? Will we lose marks for the odd inaccuracy?'

'You never know with Remnac,' Tomas said sourly.

'My point is,' Chris continued, 'that the farms

change over time, but the buildings of Portum, the craft buildings, the river, don't really change much at all, do they? Plot what we know for sure first, then put in the rest afterwards.'

Tammy and Ranya were nodding and, with a sigh, Tomas agreed and began sketching in the buildings of the Portum settlement. They had already plotted the course of the river, so it was fairly easy to add in the crafting buildings after that.

They had almost completed their map when the air was filled with a high-pitched squealing. All eyes were on Remnac, who had paled.

'A dragon has died,' he said before rushing from the room.

Immediately a murmur of conversation broke out. Chris wondered if it was the dragon who had been so badly hurt in the fight with the black dragon. He felt deep pity for the rider, whoever it was. Squeaks and warbles could be heard coming from the sleeping quarters as the young dragons emulated their elders. Almost as one, the class rose and rushed to their dragons to soothe and comfort them as best they could. Remnac found them there when he returned. He looked haggard as he leaned on the wall near the entrance to Hess's sleeping cave.

'You alright?' Chris asked, scared by the change in Remnac.

Remnac shook his head, 'The dragon that got blasted by that big black brute just died,' he said. 'You know his rider was injured too?' Chris nodded, 'Well they just had to help him cope with his dragon's death, the pain must be unbearable. He's my brother,' he added quietly.

Chris was horrified, and not surprised to see tears on Remnac's cheeks. 'I...I don't know what to say,' he whispered, clinging onto Hess. The thought of losing him suddenly more than he could bear.

Remnac shook his head and wandered off, past the other sleeping caves. Several students called out to him, but Chris heard no reply.

Having reassured Hess and watched him settle himself comfortably, Chris went to the common room and found Remnac there. Cally was with him; both were in tears. Chris poured three mugs of the ever-present batu and put two of them on the table next to his teachers. Then he took a seat at the next table and sat quietly.

Slowly, the rest of the class drifted in. All of them helped themselves to batu and silently took seats around the room. There was no conversation, just quiet companionship as they contemplated the loss of a dragon.

CHAPTER 11

The gather was to go ahead as scheduled. Signs appeared on noticeboards assuring those who wished or were able to attend that there would be no change to the plans.

Chris attended to Hess, assured him that he would be back before bedtime and bathed and changed into his tidiest clothing.

Very few of the trainees were to be allowed to the gather, and most of the riders were staying close to their dragons, so he made the walk into Portum alone. As he neared the first farm he heard his name being called. Jay and Anilla were trotting towards him, waving.

'We've been waiting for you!' Anilla squealed, throwing her arms around his neck and planting a kiss on his cheek.

Chris felt himself blushing bright red as Jay caught his eye and grinned broadly.

'Alright?' Jay said by way of greeting.

Chris nodded and allowed his friends to link arms with him and drag him along the road and into the settlement. They went past the housing and the formal, civic buildings and straight to the dining area, the hub of the village. Once they were all settled with a mug of batu and a plate of cakes and biscuits between them to share,

Anilla sat back and scrutinised Chris.

'Want to talk about it?' she asked.

Chris shrugged and shook his head. This had been a bad idea, he should have stayed with Hess, but he'd wanted to see his friends. 'I shouldn't be here,' he said hoarsely, 'I better go back.' He pushed himself to his feet but Jay put a hand on his arm.

'We know mate,' he said gently.

Chris sank back down, 'You heard it over here then?'

Jay and Anilla nodded. 'Fallaren announced it last night too,' Anilla told him, 'It's so sad.'

'Did…did you know him?' Jay asked, 'the dragon?'

'No,' Chris shook his head, 'But his rider is our teacher's brother. It's all been very sad and quiet over there. The dragons have lost their colour and all Hess wants to do is sleep.' He sighed and helped himself to a small cake, which he pulled to pieces without eating any of it.

'I'm really glad you came for the Gather,' Anilla said quietly, 'I think it'll do you good to get away for a while, and we'll walk back with you when you want to go, won't we Jay?'

Jay nodded enthusiastically, 'You should stay for a bit though,' he said, 'Edwin and Garad are dying to see you.' He grinned, 'They're full of it you know, how their first ever apprentice became a rider at his first hatching.'

'I wasn't supposed to!' Chris couldn't help smiling, 'Trust them to try taking the credit though.'

Anilla and Jay exchanged a glance before Anilla, took a deep breath. 'Can you tell us what it's really like? Having a dragon I mean. Our training is alright, but I suspect they don't tell us the half of it.' The words came out in a rush.

'Figures,' Chris said, 'a lot of my classmates are complaining they didn't know what to expect, and at least one of them has been through the training programme twice.' He finished his batu, set his mug in front of him and leaned his arms on the table with a sigh. 'I'll try to help you,' he said, 'but I don't want to scare you off, because no matter how awful and difficult I tell you it is, remember, you'll have your dragon, and that's worth anything, it's worth all the work and the aches and pains, it's even worth the hours in the classroom with Remnac.' He grinned at their astonishment.

He spent the next hour going over his first few weeks with them. He told of the problems he'd encountered, how quickly the dragons grew, how feeding them was almost an hourly ritual at first. The lessons with Remnac were in depth versions of the classes they were having now. No wonder, Chris thought, that some of his fellow students were bucking against the classroom time.

'So,' Chris sat back and looked at his friends, 'there you have it. A beginner's guide to looking after a dragon and learning how to become a true rider.'

Jay sat back his eyes wide. 'They don't tell us that!' he said, shaking his head.

'Probably they think an overview is all that's needed,' Chris suggested, 'Until you get a dragon you don't really need to know any more.'

Anilla nodded, 'I think you're right,' she said, 'but it's nice to know what we're in for, if we do get lucky.'

'Lucky?' Jay said, 'Good job we're not afraid of hard work.' He gave a half laugh.

Just then there was a crash of drums and the sounds of instruments being tuned.

Anilla winced, 'Come on, let's go for a wander around the stalls,' she said, 'We can come back later for food.'

The boys cleared the table and the three of them left the area and walked round the stalls. As they were the same as the last gather, Chris and Jay didn't have the same levels of excitement. Jay had a hotdog, Chris got himself a small pie, but he gave most of it to Jay, he had little appetite.

'I think I should head back,' he said, 'I'm not the best company today.'

As he finished speaking a heavy hand landed on his shoulder and he looked round into the broadly grinning faces of Garad and Edwin.

'Chris!' Garad boomed, 'Our very own dragon rider. How are things going with you lad?'

Everyone was turning to look at him and Chris was annoyed to feel a blush starting to grow in his face. 'I'm good thanks,' he said, more loudly than he intended.

'Your dragon grows well?' Edwin enquired.

'Yes,' Chris smiled, 'Hess is growing very well, thanks.'

'We hope you'll be back with us soon,' Garad said, 'I know most riders are able to work too, once their dragons are mature.'

'I hope so too,' Chris said, 'I miss working with you guys, I miss learning about paper and making books.' He was surprised at how much he meant what he said.

Garad and Edwin shook his hand and wished him well. Chris turned, slightly bemused, to Jay and Anilla, who were both laughing.

'I did warn you,' Jay said, 'They see Hess as a feather in their cap, certainly they see you being a rider as a lift to the esteem of the paper craft.'

Chris grinned; the meeting had cheered him a little. He was about to suggest a walk around the settlement when the warning bell began ringing. Suddenly there was pandemonium, stall holders abandoned their stalls, the people in the tents at the other side of the river were shouting and running about, unsure where they were supposed to go.

Fallaren, Narilka and a couple of other senior members of the community appeared, shouting instructions to everyone to get under cover, and fast.

Dragons appeared, wild dragons. Chris didn't know how many usually flew in attack, but there seemed to be a lot of them. He saw the leader flame, but he was too high to do any damage.

Anilla had hold of his arm now, dragging him along behind her to the big council building, but Chris wanted to watch, to see what his future held. He shook her off and watched the cliffs, waiting for Portum's dragons to appear.

They rose, hundreds of them, arranged neatly in ranks. Chris could hear the brassy calls as the dragons bellowed their fury at the intruders. He was sure the response wasn't usually this robust, perhaps it was because of the extra folk in Portum for the gather he thought.

The wild dragons turned, they flew directly towards the Portum dragons, and Chris saw blinking in action for the first time. Several ranks of dragons vanished, right before his eyes, only to reappear behind the wild dragons, behind them and beneath them. They flew, flaming at their foe, driving them higher and higher.

The wilds were surrounded on all sides by their tame counterparts. Chris watched the wilds flaming, trying to injure the dragons and their riders, he saw dragons blinking out and back again, neatly avoiding flames before issuing their own attacks. He heard the roars of the dragons, the shouts of the riders, as Portum staged a successful defence of their area and the wild dragons, a couple of them badly burned, flew higher then made their way back to wherever they lived.

'There was no black dragon,' Chris said softly to himself, 'I wonder if he died too?'

'Maybe,' A voice by his shoulder made him jump. He turned to see Fallaren standing behind him. 'Watching to see what will be expected of you?' he asked.

Chris nodded, 'I just wanted to see what happens during an attack.' He said, 'Do we normally have so many of our dragons fighting?'

'No,' Fallaren shook his head, 'but given what happened the other day, it was felt we should give a show of strength, not just for the people here, but to the wild dragons. Let them know we won't stand for it.'

Chris nodded sadly, 'I think I'd better go back,' he said, 'Hess might be unsettled and he's more important than a gather.'

Fallaren put a hand on his shoulder and gripped it firmly before giving a small shake. 'Well done lad,' he said, 'There will always be more gathers.'

'I'll just say goodbye to Anilla and Jay,' he said, as the doors of the council building burst open and people began flooding out.

Anilla and Jay found him, Anilla looked furious. 'Why did you stay outside?' she demanded.

'He just wanted to see for himself what happens,' Fallaren said, his manner easy and relaxed now that the danger was over.

Chris nodded, grinning at her, 'I think I should go though,' he said, 'Hess was really upset the other day, I can't just leave him alone now that it's happened again.'

'Ok,' Jay said, 'I understand. We'll walk back with you, if that's alright?' He looked at Fallaren, who nodded, gave Chris another gentle slap on the shoulder and walked away.

The three friends made their way through the crowds, moving against the flow of people. Eventually they were clear and Chris, eager to return to Hess, picked up his pace. When they reached the edge of the last farm holding he turned to Jay and Anilla, surprised to see them panting.

'Are you ok?' he asked.

'Yeah, we're fine,' Jay gasped, as he leaned on a fence, 'You're in a bit of a hurry that's all.'

'Sorry,' Chris looked sheepish, 'I'm just worried about...'

'Yeah, we know,' Anilla grinned, 'You go on, we'll see you soon, probably at the hatching.' Her face lit with excitement.

'Shouldn't be long now,' Jay said, 'See ya soon mate. Give that dragon a good hug from me.'

They stood and watched Chris hurry away, his walk turning into a jog.

CHAPTER 12

The next couple of days were quiet for Chris and Hess. Their flying practice continued, but Cally refused to allow them to begin blinking.

'It's really not safe at the moment,' she told a disappointed Chris the third morning after the attack, 'Hess was really shaken up by that latest attack and I feel it's best to wait a few more days. The last thing we want is an accident.'

Chris sighed, reluctant to admit she was right. 'OK,' he said slowly, 'but we won't have to wait too much longer, right?'

'No,' Cally relented with a smile, 'only a day or so.'

Chris nodded, he had been hoping to postpone his daily swimming lesson, but it wasn't to be. He was gradually improving his ability in the water, but he still wasn't confident, and Hess had needed to rescue him a few times when he got into difficulties.

He was just getting changed into his swimming gear when the dragons all began humming. The deep sound vibrated in Chris's ears unpleasantly and he shook his head, trying to rid himself of the sensation.

Cally's head snapped round towards the caves and she yelled at Chris. 'Stop, get dressed. Hatching's about to start!' She sprinted away in the direction of the classroom, reaching the huge entrance doors just as Remnac opened them and the rest of Chris's class ran out.

He pulled his clothes back on and urged Hess back towards their quarters. The class had already been informed by Remnac that their dragons were too young to attend the hatching and must be settled in their beds before their riders could leave them.

'Come on Hess,' Chris said, shoving the bronze rump before him, 'nap time.' Hess grumbled and fussed; he didn't like having been denied his swim. 'I promise I'll take you swimming later,' Chris told him, frantically changing into smarter clothing. Hess settled down and Chris stroked the smooth neck and forehead, knowing the dragon found it irresistible. A couple of minutes later Hess was asleep and Chris was racing across the floor of the bowl, desperate to get to the hatching cave before he was too late to watch Jay and Anilla.

Once in the cave he took the steps two at a time up the seating tiers, looking for a place to sit. Everywhere was full.

'Psst. Hey, Midget!' He saw Nat on his left, she was sitting with Dar and a couple of other riders he didn't know. 'Come on,' she beckoned to him, 'There's a space here.'

Chris made his way to her and plonked down in the seat next to Nat. Dar leaned around her to slap him on the knee. 'Thought you weren't going to make it.'

'Wouldn't miss it for the world,' Chris said, 'Two of my friends are trying for a dragon.'

As he finished speaking a line of youngsters were led in by a rider. Chris fairly bounced in his seat when he spotted Jay, Anilla right behind him. They looked pale and nervous, but Jay waved enthusiastically when he spotted Chris, pointing him out to Anilla, who gave him a weak smile before returning her attention to the eggs on the sand.

This was a smaller clutch than the last one, Chris counted ten eggs, but the buzz of excitement was the same. Narilka and Fallaren walked in to take their seats. They were followed by several of Chris's classmates, who scurried up the steps looking for seats.

The eggs were rocking as the baby dragons inside began their fight for freedom. The tension in the cave grew as the first cracks appeared in the shells. It seemed to take forever for the first dragon to emerge. Small, damp and with translucent skin, the youngster tumbled out of the remnants of its shell and struggled to its feet. As it made its clumsy way towards the waiting line of hopefuls a second dragon managed to break its shell open.

The first baby had fallen at the feet of a young man, who was now stroking the creature and encouraging it to stand. Nat nudged Chris sharply in the ribs and pointed to a row of seats two in front of them. Chris saw Rampton the Tanner, beaming with pride, the new rider must be his son. Chris hoped he wasn't like his father or Remnac would have his hands full.

The second dragon, bigger than the first, was now perusing the youngsters. It took its time, standing before a couple of lads, who got their hopes up, before finally rejecting them. Then it came to Jay and Chris held his breath. He watched the dragon dip its head, then it nudged Jay with its nose and Chris saw the joyful expression of Jay's face as he reached towards his own dragon for the first time. Chris was shocked to discover tears rolling down his cheeks and he hurriedly rubbed them away, wiping his eyes on his sleeve, not wanting to miss a moment.

Most of the remaining eggs were rocking now, and three dragons escaped from their shells at the same time. They all wobbled towards the waiting line and were paired up quickly with their delighted new riders. Chris wondered if they would still be delighted in a couple of weeks when the reality of looking after a dragon hit them.

Another dragon was making its way towards the line, feebly attempting to flap its wings. It stopped short of Anilla and Chris found his heart in his mouth as he watched the baby, but it chose the girl standing next to her.

At last there were just two eggs left on the sand. A large one which was rocking robustly, and a smaller one which was making no movement at all. All attention was on the lively egg now, as huge cracks appeared in the shell, splitting it in half. The dragon within flopped out onto the sand, crying and squawking. Getting to its feet, it shook itself and tried to flip damp wings to its back before walking towards the remaining hopefuls. This dragon knew exactly who it wanted. It walked straight up to Anilla and butted against her with its head, demanding attention.

This time Chris couldn't hide his tears. He felt Nat putting her arm round his shoulders and giving him a squeeze. 'You ok Midget?' she whispered.

Chris could only nod. Someone passed him a handkerchief, which he took gratefully, wiping his eyes and blowing his nose. 'My friend.' He said at last, indicating Anilla. Her dragon was starting to dry now and the scales were showing tints of gold.

'It's always emotional at a hatching,' Nat said, 'Always get me too, you can't help remembering what it feels like, how special it is. I'm glad your mates got dragons. If they're anything like you, Remnac is going to be happy with them.'

Chris looked round, surprised but happy. 'Thanks,' he said, trying hard not to sniff. 'What's going to happen with the other egg?' he asked, indicating the sand where the smallest egg lay.

'Nothing I suppose,' Nat shrugged, 'doesn't look like it's going to hatch now. We do get the odd dud.'

'Oh.' Chris felt sad for the little egg, left all alone. He hoped whoever got the job of cleaning up would treat it gently. He was looking for Jay now among the crowds, he caught a glimpse of his friend as he made his way with his new partner towards the back of the cave where the dragons would be fed. 'Do you think they'd mind if I went down to see the new dragons?' he asked Nat.

'We're not supposed to,' she told him, 'But as they're your friends it might be ok. I mean, it's Remnac down there with them, how bad can he be? You're his star pupil right now, he might want to parade you as a good example, he doesn't get many of those.' She grinned cheekily at him before giving his shoulder a shove. 'Off you go then. See ya later Midget.'

Chris scampered down the steps and onto the sands, wanting to follow his friends and congratulate them, but he found himself held back by a strong arm across his shoulders.

'Where are you off to?'

Chris looked up into Garad's face and grinned. 'I was going to see your other apprentice,' he said, 'You want to watch it, the paper crafters will get a reputation for apprentices becoming riders.'

'Aye, Edwin and me are real proud of you lads. I'm sure we'll manage till you're ready to come back. How is that young hooligan of yours getting on?'

'Hooligan? Hess is fine thank you.' Chris was initially shocked that Garad would think about a dragon that way, then realised Jay would have told him the tales of the young bronze and his headstrong ways. 'He takes some handling, but he's going to be a strong flyer. Has a mind of his own though, I do have a bit of trouble with him,' He admitted ruefully.

'I heard,' Garad laughed, 'Go on, go find young Jay, and tell him congratulations from us too, will you?'

Chris nodded and darted away before anyone else could stop him. He trotted into the back cave and soon found Jay, who was having trouble stopping his dragon sticking its head into the bucket. Chris grabbed the bucket and held it away from the baby. Jay's head whipped round, and his hands reached for the bucket, then he saw Chris and relaxed.

'Let me help,' Chris said, 'I know what this is like. They're so greedy.'

'Thanks,' Jay said, reaching into the bucket and offering the small pieces of meat to his dragon, whose scales were now drying nicely, showing shades of brown with red glimmering beneath.

'He's going to be handsome, isn't he?' Chris said, 'I can't get over how small they are, Hess looks huge compared to these guys.'

'They grow fast though, at first, don't they?' Jay replied, trying to stop his dragon from eating all the meat at once. 'You'll choke yourself,' he said sternly, 'one bit at a time please.'

'What's his name?' Chris asked.

'Name? I dunno, haven't had time to think of one,' Jay said, hurriedly grabbing more meat for the hungry dragon.

'They already have names,' Chris laughed, 'Do you really think I'd have come up with Hessarion on my own?'

'Oh. I didn't know that.' Jay looked thoughtfully at his new companion, 'Come on then, what's your name?'

Chris watched the pair as they communicated without words, remembering how strange it had felt to him at first.

'He says his name is Sorbus,' Jay's eyes were wide and he automatically stroked the rapidly drying neck, gazing at his dragon. 'Isn't he beautiful?'

'He is.' A deep voice behind them made the boys jump and they looked round to see Fallaren watching them. 'Lending a hand young Chris?'

'Yeah,' Chris felt himself growing hot, 'I wanted to congratulate Jay and Anilla, but he was struggling so, you know...' he shrugged and held up the bucket.

'I'll take over now,' Remnac bustled up, 'young lady

over there is asking for you lad.'

'Anilla?' Chris handed the bucket to Remnac, 'where is she?'

'Just over there,' Remnac waved vaguely and Chris set off to find his friend.

He spotted the dragon before he saw Anilla, the pale gold of her scales gleamed in the dull light of the cave. 'Hey,' he said, jogging up to the pair, 'How are you feeling?'

Anilla looked up at him, her eyes glowing. 'Isn't this wonderful?' she whispered, 'I've never felt like this before. Hayvor is stunning, isn't she?'

'She's beautiful,' Chris agreed, 'It's a wonderful feeling, isn't it?'

Anilla just nodded as she fed her new friend. 'I can't believe it,' she said quietly, 'My first time of trying and look!'

'Were any of your family able to watch?' Chris asked.

'Well, my cousins were here, not sure if my parents made it,' she told him, 'But they'll be so proud.' She wasn't having the same struggle with feeding that Jay was enduring. Hayvor had good manners.

'I've just seen Jay,' Chris told her, 'His dragon is playing up, trying to eat all his food at once. Hayvor is much better behaved.'

'Of course she is,' Anilla said at once, 'She's perfect.' Beside her the golden dragon shook her head and rubbed up against her rider, asking for attention. Anilla immediately stroked the soft nose, nuzzling against

Hayvor's neck.

'I'll leave you to it,' Chris said, backing away. 'See you later Anilla, Hayvor.' He turned and made his way back across the cave to Jay, who had now finished feeding Sorbus.

Remnac was demanding the attention of all the new riders now, Chris gave Jay a quick smile before darting out of the cave and back into the main hatching cavern. Folk were picking up the remnants of shells which had been scattered around, the small egg was still in its place. He wandered over to it and was about to put his hand on it when Fallaren's voice stopped him.

'Chris. Don't touch it, we've yet to discover if it's live or not.'

'Will touching it do anything?' Chris asked, recalling how he had touched the shell of Hess's egg before he hatched.

'We're not sure,' Fallaren admitted, 'but best not to take risks.'

As he spoke a couple of men arrived, their pins announced them as healers, and they carefully placed a listening contraption to the egg, bending close to detect any sounds. After a few minutes the stood and shook their heads, there were no signs of life from the egg.

Sadly, Chris walked away and headed back to Hess, who he knew would be ready for his meal by now. He kicked at the gravel as he walked, wondering why he was so sad that the little egg hadn't hatched.

CHAPTER 13

Over the next few days, Chris caught only fleeting glimpses of his friends as they got to grips with caring for their new companions. He was busy himself, with morning flying and swimming sessions with Cally and lessons with Remnac in the afternoons. Cally was still holding back from teaching them how to blink.

'Hess is still shaken by the attack, and then the hatching coming so soon afterwards,' she told Chris, 'It always leaves the dragons feeling strange for a while and I don't want to risk you two getting yourselves lost.'

'We wouldn't!' Chris said hotly, 'I would never take risks with Hess.'

'Good, then you'll be happy to wait until he's settled again.' Cally smiled triumphantly.

Chris sighed and gave in, changing into his swimming gear for today's lesson.

***

At lunch later that day, Chris and the rest of his class were sitting in the common room. Chris was listening to the latest list of complaints from Ranya, most of which centred around Remnac, who was attempting to teach them advanced dragon care. The doors flew open, and the newest class of riders entered the room, chattering loudly. Jay and Anilla immediately spotted Chris, waving and grinning at him as they went to help themselves to lunch. Their group all seemed to be getting along, but Jay and Anilla got their food and came to sit by Chris rather than sitting with their peers.

'Hey,' Jay said, plonking himself down next to Chris, 'How's it going?'

'Oh, you know,' Chris said with a sigh, 'Still too much work to do. Hess is brilliant, but he gets to sleep as much as he wants. I have lessons with Remnac.'

'How long does this hungry period last?' Anilla wanted to know, 'Hayvor's a bottomless pit, she's as bad as you were Chris, when you first got to Portum.'

Chris grinned, 'You've got weeks yet,' he said, 'before long they'll have you down in the kitchens chopping her meat up yourself. You'll love Felix.'

Across the table, Ranya snorted and Tammy hit her a couple of times between the shoulder blades. 'Felix is wonderful, isn't he?' Ranya managed at last.

Jay and Anilla cast nervous glances at each other.

'It's ok,' Chris said, 'Felix works in the butchery department, it's his job to teach us all how to prepare the meat for the dragons and he's not very cheerful about it. You'll be alright if you pay attention though.'

'Butchery?' Anilla looked horrified.

'Yeah,' Ranya nodded at her cousin, 'it's awful, and the smell!' She waved her hand beneath her nose. Next to her, Tammy nodded, her face screwed up in distaste. 'If it weren't for Tathdel, I'd go nowhere near the kitchens. At least we don't have to do it forever, just till they're big enough to get their own food.'

'If it weren't for Tathdel, you wouldn't need to go near the kitchens,' Chris pointed out.

Ranya pouted and lowered her face. Chris glanced at Anilla who winked at him. Shocked, Chris looked to Jay sat on his other side. Jay shrugged, busily chewing his lunch.

Remnac appeared in the doorway and called the place to order. 'I need my class back in the lecture room as soon as possible please. Lots to do this afternoon.'

With loud groans Chris and his classmates stood up, stacked plates and prepared for lessons.

'Enjoy,' Anilla said, 'perhaps we'll catch up with you later?'

'Yeah, hopefully,' Chris said, knowing it was unlikely with the amount of extra work Remnac was piling onto them, determined they would all pass and progress to their squads before there could be another hatching.

That night Chris determined to push Cally in the morning, he was fed up of waiting to advance with Hess. He wanted to know all the tricks there were to this flying game. He wanted to be promoted to a squad as soon as possible, wanted to be useful to Portum to pay back the kindness he had been shown since he arrived. He rehearsed his speech late into the night, making what he hoped were relevant points which would make Cally reconsider her stance on Hess and himself learning to blink.

***

The following morning, bleary eyed and yawning widely, Chris followed Hess across the bowl to Cally and Fin.

'Well, don't you look full of beans today,' Cally greeted him cheerily.

Chris grunted. His head ached, not even the three cups of batu he'd swallowed with his breakfast had revived him.

'Well, I hope you're more awake than you look,' Cally continued, 'I was hoping to get you and young Hess to give blinking a try.'

Chris, who was busily fastening the harness onto Hess, looked up at her in amazement. He could have saved himself a sleepless night!

'Great,' he managed, 'I was hoping we'd get to it sooner rather than later.'

'Well, Rem had a bit of a go at me last night,' Cally admitted, 'and I must admit, you two have been the perfect pupils...more or less. So I can't hold you back any longer. Meet me over the other side of the lake as soon as you're ready.' She vaulted to her seat on Fin's neck, and they took off, Fin skimming low over the lake to land neatly on the other side.

Chris felt excitement bubbling in his stomach as he finished fastening the harness and checked all the straps. He couldn't give Cally any excuses now. He climbed up onto Hess's shoulder and settled himself as comfortably as he could before giving Hess the order to join their teachers.

Hess leapt into the air, his wings beat twice, and

they were following Fin's example, soaring across the lake. The wind in his face revived Chris, he loved flying. Hess landed facing Cally and Fin, neatly folding his wings across his back as he and Chris waited eagerly for their next instructions.

'You remember these I presume?' Cally indicated the patterns of pebbles. Chris nodded. 'Good. Are you sure you've got the exact pattern memorised?'

Chris looked at the stones before them, making sure the intricate pattern was lodged firmly in his memory. He nodded.

'Right, now I want you and Hess to fly to the rock where the river comes into the Portum area.' Cally said, 'And when you're there, you pause, you visualise these stones as clearly as you can,' she pointed to them, 'and you give that image to Hess. Then you ask him to take you there. Or here.' She laughed a little nervously.

'OK, we can do that.' Chris said, eager to be off.

Cally gave him the nod and Hess lifted off again, circling the lake once before heading down towards the far end of the Portum settlement.

Once they were at the rock, Hess hovered. Chris visualised the pattern of stones as clearly as he could. 'Got it Hess?' he whispered against the roar of the wind in his ears. Hess rumbled. 'Then take us there please.'

Everything went dark, the river and mountains, the village all melted into one and Chris felt as if he were being stretched to the very edge of his limits, while at the same time being squashed flat. There was a popping sound and he and Hess were back where they started, in front of Cally and Fin who were looking nervously at them.

'Well done!' Cally yelled with more enthusiasm than Chris had ever heard from her.

'Thanks.' Chris felt very green. He slipped down from Hess and stumbled over to some rocks where he quietly threw up his breakfast.

Returning to Hess he found Cally standing next to the bronze, she offered him a water bottle which he accepted gratefully, drinking deeply.

'Is that normal?' he asked at last, leaning against Hess and pushing his damp hair out of his eyes.

'Perfectly,' Cally said, 'I'd say almost all the riders who manage this trick experience the sickness thing for the first few times.'

'Great.' Chris said with feeling, 'and you didn't warn me because?'

'I didn't want to inhibit you in any way,' Cally said, 'you and Hess needed to give it your full attention without you worrying about what may or may not happen afterwards.'

'Fair enough I suppose,' Chris groaned. 'What's next then?'

'Today? Nothing much for you.' Cally said firmly, 'I think we'll fly over to the next village to stretch Hess's wings and let you see their layout so you can practice blinking to and from there over the next few days. We'll take things slowly though, don't want to overtire him, or you,' she added hurriedly when Chris looked at her with raised eyebrows. 'When you're ready, mount up and we'll get off.'

Chris clambered back up onto his seat and fastened the flying straps. Once he was ready, he nodded sharply at Cally and both dragons leapt for the sky.

***

That afternoon the lessons with Remnac dragged. Chris had to keep himself awake and it was a struggle. All he could think about was his bed. Hess was slumbering peacefully now, and when Chris reached out with his mind to his dragon, he caught sleepy dreams of flying. He forced his attention back to Remnac and what should have been an interesting lesson on flying formations in battle.

Glancing over at Tomas next to him he was pleased to see pages of notes. Perhaps Tomas would allow him to read through them later and copy down the important bits.

Tomas caught his eye and grinned at him. 'You look well tired,' he whispered under the cover of his hand as he leaned towards Chris, 'bad morning?'

Chris nodded, 'Bad night too mate,' he said with a groan.

'I'll lend you my notes,' Tomas said softly, 'no worries.'

'Thanks,' Chris said, hurriedly scribbling down what Remnac was saying hoping he hadn't missed anything important.

***

That evening Chris sat in the common room making notes from the sheets Tomas had handed him.

'You looked like you were about to fall asleep this

afternoon,' Tomas said, coming to sit beside him.

'I was,' Chris said with a groan, wiping his hand over his face. 'Bad night, followed by a heavy morning with the flying stuff. I just want my bed.' He gave a half laugh before returning to the notes. He was glad Tomas had neat writing, and the boy wrote down everything! Ten minutes later he reached the point where he had started making his own coherent notes and handed them back to Tomas. 'Thanks Tom, I really appreciate it.'

'No problem.' Tomas grinned, 'I wish everyone would call me Tom,' he looked around the busy room, 'but they all insist on my full name. I thought all riders contracted their names to make it easier to shout instructions in battle, but this lot...'

Chris thought for a moment before nodding slowly. 'Yeah, the riders I've met have all shortened their names.' He said, 'Cally calls Remnac Rem, and Nat and Dar have definitely shortened theirs. Only ones I know who use their full names are Fallaren and Narilka, and I bet they have short forms for when they fly.'

'Exactly.' Tomas said vehemently.

'So tell 'em,' Chris said, 'next time someone calls you Tomas,' he mimicked Ranya's voice perfectly, eliciting a loud laugh from Tom, 'tell her you'd prefer it if she called you Tom and see what reaction you get.'

Chris rose to put his notes somewhere safe while the newly re-named Tom wandered casually across to the group containing Ranya. Chris paused to watch. He heard Ranya greet Tomas, heard his deeper voice requesting the nick name and saw Ranya become flustered, turning bright red. Grinning to himself, Chris wandered to his sleeping quarters, edging past Hess, who was fast asleep in his own chamber, to store his notes on the shelf he used for all his schoolwork. Nat was right, he thought, he and Hess were going to require more space soon. Hess was growing so quickly; he'd be fully grown in a few months. Chris knew the growth spurt would soon slow, thanks to Remnac's lectures, and full size would be attained by the dragons approximately eighteen months after they'd hatched. He stood for a moment watching his sleeping dragon, wondering just how much bigger Hess would get. He reached out a gentle hand and stroked the soft nose, before returning to the common room for more batu. He was hoping to see Jay and Anilla as he sauntered to the table to get himself a drink. While his back was turned to the room the noise level rose significantly as the newest recruits appeared. Chris barely managed to turn around before Anilla and Jay were there, looking tired but happy.

'What happened to you the other night?' Jay demanded.

'Remnac.' Chris responded with a grimace.

'Ah, homework getting too much for you, is it?' Anilla asked, no trace of sympathy in her voice.

'No.' Chris said a little more loudly than he'd intended. 'Sorry. No, it's not too much, it's me. I push myself because I desperately want this stage to be over with, and Rem told us we can't graduate to a squad until we pass all his classes.' His unconscious use of Remnac's shortened name raised Anilla's eyebrows but she said nothing.

'So you're doing the same thing you did when

you started learning how to make paper?' Jay asked cheerfully.

'Yep,' Chris grinned at his friends, 'it's all my own fault, but not really. How are you two getting on?'

Twin groans told him everything he needed to know.

'Shall we get a table?' Jay asked, glancing around the busy room. 'There's one, right at the back. Come on.' He darted away, leaving Anilla and Chris to make their way towards the table he'd indicated. Chris couldn't help noticing the similarities to his life in Salutem, but he shook himself. At least here he got to go outside every day.

'Are you alright Chris?' Anilla's hand lightly touched his arm, concern lit her face.

'Yeah, I'm fine,' he said in a determined tone, 'just having flashbacks to Salutem.'

'Salutem was like this?'

'No, not really, but this room,' he waved his free arm, 'is very like the entertainment area back there. We spent every evening in that place, playing cards and plotting our escape. Shame we didn't all make it. Not sure what Portum would make of Baz though.' He gave a small laugh at the thought.

'Baz?'

'One of my mates. She's er...' Chris chose his words carefully, 'a bit different from other girls.'

'Oh?' Anilla queried as she took a seat at the table.

'Yeah, she's a bit of a rogue,' Chris grinned, imagining Baz's reaction to his choice of words. 'She got into a fight with the guards and lost a tooth. You should have seen the other guy though, I heard he couldn't walk straight for a month.'

'Wow,' Jay looked stunned, 'shame she didn't get out with you guys, I imagine she'd have livened things up a bit round here.'

'That's one way of putting it!' Chris grinned.

Anilla looked concerned. 'How many youngsters are there in your cave systems?' she asked.

'I dunno,' Chris responded helpfully, 'around my age? Maybe forty or so, why?'

'Same for Barlang,' Jay informed her.

The boys looked inquisitively at Anilla, who sat looking at the table, seemingly intent on memorising the pattern of the wood.

'Should I go get us some more batu?' Jay asked cheerfully.

'Yeah, I reckon so mate,' Chris said softly. Once Jay had departed, he reached across the table and lightly touched Anilla's arm. 'What's going on?' he asked.

The contact startled Anilla and she looked up. 'Nothing, nothing really,' she said, sounding confused. 'I was just thinking, wondering really, about population numbers and so on.'

Chris looked confused and was about to ask more questions when Jay returned bearing a large jug and three mugs. 'Supplies!' he announced happily, setting everything on the table and pouring drinks for each of them.

Anilla did her best to shake herself out of her strange mood and the evening became the usual conversation, peppered with bad jokes and laughter.

Chris yawned widely and looked at the huge clock which hung above the doorway. 'Half past nine,' he stated, 'must be getting old but I feel like it's bedtime for me.'

'Yeah, probably a good idea,' Jay agreed, 'tomorrow's another super busy day after all.'

Slowly they cleared their table and made their way to their respective beds. Anilla still quietly thoughtful.

CHAPTER 14

Chris didn't have time to muse over Anilla's comments. The following days were filled with excitement as the entire class moved outside to commence flying lessons. Suddenly, Chris didn't have Cally's undivided attention.

He and Hess were much in advance when it came to flying, soaring happily high above Portum and the surrounding villages while the rest were subjected to the same lessons he had received weeks ago. He was grateful for his swimming lessons when he realised he could hold his own with the rest of his classmates and he began to enjoy his sessions in the lake with Hess.

Afternoon lessons had taken on a new element now that the whole class were experiencing the morning flying and bathing sessions. Twice Ranya fell asleep in the classroom and had to be nudged awake by Tammy. Even Tate and Tom were yawing widely by mid-afternoon. Remnac showed them no mercy, continuing with his intense lessons, much as he had when it was Chris yawning and struggling to stay awake.

At the end of the first week, Ranya found Chris in the common room and plonked herself down opposite him with a sigh.

'Alright,' she said moodily, 'how did you do it?'

'Do what?' Chris was bemused.

'Manage the flying and swimming and bathing and then lessons without falling asleep and drooling on your desk?'

Chris grinned. 'Well,' he said, 'I made sure I drank plenty of batu…'

'Yeah, we noticed you were downing the stuff.'

'And I got good at hiding my yawns. Also, Tom takes fantastic notes and he let me see them if I zoned out during Remnac's lectures.' He grinned at her. 'Not as much fun as you thought, is it?'

'Humph!' Ranya put her arms on the table and let her head droop.

'It gets easier, or rather you get used to it,' Chris said more kindly, 'but these first few weeks are tough. Go to bed earlier so you get enough rest and try to make things as easy for yourself as you can.'

'How?'

'Well,' Chris cocked his head on one side as he thought, 'I always put everything ready for the next morning before I go to bed, that way I don't forget anything vital while I'm still half asleep. I guess it's just better to be organised. No point doing your hair if you're going flying cos it'll only be ruined, plus you'll be in the lake later, so leave the hair in a braid and sort it out later. That kind of thing.'

'Thanks.' Ranya said, nodding slowly. 'I see what you mean, I'll give it a try.' She rose from the table. 'Guess it's an early bedtime for me for a while.' She gave him a half smile and wandered across the common room to the table Tammy was sitting at.

Chris watched her leave with a tired smile on his face, he understood, he really did, but he didn't have a quick fix for her, for any of them. They all had to go through the process and simply get used to the extra tasks being put on them. The alternative didn't bear thinking about. He drained his mug of batu and was about to leave when a hand landed on his shoulder. He looked round into Jay's cheery face.

'Hi, how's things?' Jay asked, sitting down in the seat recently vacated by Ranya.

'Oh, you know,' Chris knew he sounded grumpy, but he was tired. The morning flight had been longer than usual while Cally and Fin attended to the new flyers.

'I wanted to talk to you,' Jay said, suddenly serious.

Chris sat up, Jay being serious was unusual. 'What's up?'

'Anilla.' Jay said quietly, looking over his shoulder to make sure they weren't being overheard.

'What about her?'

'You remember the conversation we all had the other night? When she was asking about numbers in Salutem and Barlang?'

Chris nodded, 'yeah.' He wondered where this was going.

'Mate, I think she's planning on going there, getting folk out.'

'What?' Chris said far more loudly than he'd intended. Heads were turning in their direction now and he glanced around, smiling weakly, before returning his attention to his friend. 'You can't be serious. She can't be serious. It's not possible.'

Jay shrugged. 'I still think she's got it in her head,' he said. 'She's been very quiet ever since, always seems deep in thought when I talk to her, like I've interrupted something important.'

Chris felt his stomach drop at the thought of Anilla putting herself in such danger. 'If it were possible to do that, then surely Fallaren would have done it by now, or at least tried.' He said quietly.

'You'd think so, wouldn't you?' Jay agreed.

'Is there really such a shortage of folk round here?' Chris was confused. 'Portum always seems so busy, how can they be short of people to have dragons?'

'I think they need younger folk; can you imagine Garad or Edwin doing what we're doing?' Jay said.

They both laughed loudly, no longer caring if people looked at them. Chris had tears running down his cheeks and Jay could hardly breathe, he was leaning on the table, shoulders shaking with laughter.

'What's so funny?' Anilla had appeared. She sat next to Chris, looking at the pair in baffled amusement.

'Just thinking about Garad and Edwin with dragons,' Chris gasped, setting Jay off again.

'What on earth made you think about that?' Anilla sounded cool, more distant than usual.

'Just talking about running out of people for new dragons, that's all.' Jay said, taking a sip of batu as he tried to get control of himself.

'And you thought Edwin and Garad?' Anilla said faintly, but she smiled.

'Well, you know, if they were desperate,' Chris said, which set Jay off laughing again.

Anilla shook her head. 'Boys…' she said in disbelief.

'You started it,' Chris told her.

'I did?' Anilla looked puzzled, 'I wasn't even here.'

'No, with what you said the other night. You know, about numbers in Salutem and Barlang. Set us off wondering, that's all.'

'Oh.' Anilla said softly.

Chris and Jay sobered instantly. 'How badly do we need new people?' Jay asked.

'It depends.' Anilla replied quietly, 'on how soon the next female's flight is, on how many eggs are laid, how many more make it out of the various cave systems and get to Portum and how quickly any newcomers can be ready for a dragon. You,' she nudged Chris, 'are very unusual you know, not many can come out of the caves and adjust so well to life outside. We've had some who took years before they were comfortable with sky instead of a roof.'

'No female has flown recently, have they? I mean, not since the last clutch was laid.' Jay asked thoughtfully.

'No,' Anilla said, 'but dragons…who knows?'

Chris sat in silence, chewing his lower lip. Jay trotted off and brought batu for them all. The group sat quietly while they sipped their drinks. This was unusual enough that Ranya, Tammy and Tom noticed. Eventually,

Tom rose from their table and sauntered over to Chris and his friends.

'Hey,' he said in a cheerful way, 'you three alright? Never seen you so quiet?'

Chris jumped as Tom spoke. 'Yeah, I think so,' he said, looking up into Tom's face, 'just tired, you know?'

Tom nodded. 'I know mate,' he said, 'if there's anything I can do, you let me know, right?'

Chris nodded, 'Thanks Tom, appreciate that.'

'Breakthrough.' Jay said softly, 'looks like progress is being made with your class then?'

'Yeah,' Chris said quietly, picking up his mug to cover what he was saying, 'they're all outside flying every day now, they understand how I've been feeling, that I was trying to help them, not bragging about what I was doing.'

'I should think not!' Anilla was horrified, 'you would never do something like that.'

'Yeah mate,' Jay added, 'you're just not like that.'

'I know that, and you know that, but they,' Chris jerked a thumb in the direction of his classmates, 'don't know me at all. Well, they didn't, seems they want to get to know me now.' He yawned widely. 'Think it's about bedtime for me, got flying again in the morning. See you guys tomorrow.' He heaved himself to his feet and sauntered towards Hess and his comfortable bed.

CHAPTER 15

'Attention please!' Remnac stood at the front of the classroom and tapped on his desk. Gradually the room fell silent, even Ranya was overcome by curiosity and stopped her giggling, paying attention to their instructor.

'This,' Remnac waved a scroll in the air once he was sure he held the attention of the class, 'is a listing of the current squads, their names, colours and badges. I need you all to know them. Soon you will be graduating to a squad of your own and knowing the names of all the squads will be expected of you. When you fly against the wilds you need to know who's who up there, who is your teammate, who you can call on to back you up if necessary.' He unrolled the scroll and moved to the board, chalk in hand.

In his clear handwriting, he began listing all the flying squads of Portum, the class obediently copied them down. This was more interesting than history at least, this meant something for their future.

Remnac wrote: *Crow – Black; Eagle – Tan; Osprey – Grey; Magpie – Blue; Swan – White; Kestrel – Brown; Starling – Green; Kingfisher – Turquoise; Bullfinch – Orange; Curlew – Red; Mallard – Yellow.*

Once he'd finished writing Remnac waited for a few moments as the class caught up, then he continued.

'Each squad has their own pin, much as you received when you entered your crafts. Also, when flying you will each have your own flying jacket which bears your squad affiliation on the back and both sleeves.' A ripple of murmurs ran round the room at this news and Remnac could feel the excitement emanating from the group.

Chris recalled the jacket Nat usually wore; it made more sense to him now. She was in, he checked his list, Osprey because her jacket had grey patches on the sleeves and the back was decorated with a grey shield, within which was the silhouette of a bird, which Chris now presumed was the Osprey. He wondered idly which squad he would be assigned to.

Ranya's hand was in the air, 'Remnac, excuse me, do we get to choose which squad we'd like to be in?'

Beside her Tammy was nodding and looking hopeful.

'No,' Remnac shook his head, 'sorry ladies, but you get put where we feel you will be best suited. Some squads have specialisms you see,' he continued when their faces fell, 'and we must make sure that the right riders and dragons are in the best place.'

'Oh.' Ranya's face was alight with curiosity now. 'What specialisms? Does Tathy have any?'

Remnac grinned. 'We haven't finalised the lists yet,' he told her. 'We'll let you all know as soon as you're ready to progress, but please be patient, you still have work to do. This lesson is all part of preparing you though, for life beyond this classroom.'

At break that afternoon the group were much happier than normal. Everyone sat together, discussing the merits and otherwise of each squad Remnac had told them about.

'I hope I'm in Kingfisher,' Tammy said, 'they sound really good, fast dragons, in and out of places at speed.' Tammy and her green, Priyan, had taken to flying well and were now known for their speed and agility.

Chris wasn't too bothered where he was put, it seemed to him that there was little point in worrying about it as Remnac and whoever else was responsible for the decision would only look at how he and Hess worked together, weigh in any skills they possessed as a pair, and put them where they thought best. It wouldn't matter what his opinion was so why bother forming one?

While they were finishing off their batu a strange noise vibrated through the caves. Heads were shaken and puzzled looks exchanged before Remnac came running in looking more panicked than they had ever seen.

'Go to your dragons.' He shouted, 'keep them calm, distract them with food. Sariba has risen to mate, it will unsettle them.'

The class ran from the room and towards their dragons, grabbing buckets of meat as they went. Down the corridor came the calls of confusion and distress from the young dragons.

Chris reached Hess to find him on his haunches, neck stretched out, hooting and crying. He reached for the soft hide of the neck to stroke and was shocked when Hess lowered his head and hissed at him. Grabbing his hand back, he felt in the bucket and pulled out a chunk of meat. 'Alright Hess? Fancy a snack?' Hess gave a huge hiccup and sniffed at the meat. For the first time in his life, he refused food, although he did settle down a little. Chris stood for a moment, watching as Hess moved agitatedly on his bed, head swaying back and forth. 'It's ok Hess, it's only Sariba, and probably Neldor. You're safe, it's ok mate.' The soothing tone seemed to calm the young dragon, and he reached out to nuzzle his rider. Cautiously, Chris lifted his hand and stroked the neck and soft muzzle, making soft noises all the while until Hess was properly settled and showing interest in the bucket.

Chris lifted the bucket and picked up the piece of meat again. This time Hess decided food was more important than whatever those grown-up dragons were getting up to. Chris fed him the meat one piece at a time, making sure he stroked and comforted the bronze in between mouthfuls.

Suddenly noise exploded around him as all the young dragons called at the same time. Hess rose on his haunches, rearing high above his rider, and the noise that came from him shocked Chris. A great, deep bellow reverberated around the stone walls. He looked up at Hess in surprise, but Hess ignored him and continued bellowing. Nothing Chris could do worked; the agitated dragon was caught up in whatever was going on outside. Chris reached out to him with his mind but only caught chaotic thoughts of flight and many dragons. Surely the wilds weren't attacking during the flight of the queen.

As his quarters were closest to the doors to the bowl, he crept closer and was about to pull the door open a little to peep out when a firm hand yanked him backwards.

'Get back to your dragon.' Remnac's voice vibrated with anger.

Shocked, Chris returned to Hess, who was starting to calm down now. He tentatively reached for the soft hide of the chest, ready to snatch his hand away if Hess reacted badly, but the dragon allowed the contact, settling down onto his forelegs again. He was still grumbling, but much calmer by the time Remnac appeared.

'Sorry about that.' Remnac said in much calmer tones.

'What was happening?' Chris asked.

'Sariba went up, always causes a lot of excitement among the dragons as she's the head female. Neldor was with her, naturally, they're a bonded pair. Things were just calming down again when the wilds appeared, the excitement must have attracted them. That nasty black brute was with them again. Could still see where he was injured last time. Anyway, he went for Sariba and Neldor. The Portum dragons didn't wait for their riders, they attacked him.'

Chris gasped. 'I thought they didn't fly without riders.'

'They don't,' Remnac said grimly, 'but this all happened so fast there was no time to wait.'

'Have we any casualties?' Chris whispered.

'I don't think so. We do have some angry riders though. However, our bronzes chased this black dragon out of Portum, flaming him all the way, I understand. He won't be back any time soon, his wings and tail were badly damaged. He barely managed to get back to the cliffs where they're nesting.'

'So we know where they live now?'

'Yes. For all the good it'll do us.' Remnac said savagely and Chris wondered if he thought pro-active attacks were the way to go. 'Young Hess found his voice today, didn't he?' Remnac continued in a lighter tone, giving the bronze dragon a slap.

'He certainly did,' Chris said, 'bet I'll have trouble getting him to shut up now though.' He gave a half laugh, leaning against the bronze foreleg. Hess looked at his rider, bumping him with his nose. 'More food?' Chris enquired, picking up the almost empty bucket. 'You almost ate it all, but here,' he picked up a piece of meat and tossed it in the air. Hess caught it, his jaws snapping as they closed around the food. He swallowed and looked hopefully at Chris.

'He seems back to normal then.' Remnac said, 'see you back in class as soon as you're done here.'

'Of course.' Chris said, tipping out the rest of the meat for Hess to help himself to. He stroked the top of his head gently, his thoughts miles away.

Gradually the class reassembled in the teaching room. Whispered, worried conversations hissed around the room as the young riders attempted to make sense of what had just happened. Remnac appeared and called the class to order.

'I need to tell you all that all is well,' he began, 'although the wilds were attracted by the commotion of Sariba rising, they were seen off with no casualties on our part. Now, back to our lesson. Squads and the role you will each be expected to play when you graduate.'

There were groans from around the room, but the

class settled down to notetaking. At least this lesson had a direct impact on their immediate future life in Portum.

CHAPTER 16

Hess was now very fond of his own voice. He announced his presence in the bowl each morning as he and Chris went out for their daily flying sessions. The pair were required to be out first so Cally could give them coordinates for them to work on blinking. They were coming along slowly, but Chris still felt nauseous each time they attempted the feat, he was starting to think he wouldn't be able to continue.

'I can't be like this if we're fighting, can I?' he wailed to Cally, 'stopping every five minutes to throw up.' He sighed heavily and thumped Hess on the shoulder. The dragon rumbled in disapproval. 'Sorry Hess, it's not your fault.'

'I admit, you're taking longer than I expected to get used to it,' Cally said, 'but I'm sure you'll be just fine if you keep practising. One jump a day is all you need.' She gave him the destination for the day and sent them off.

'Right Hess, got where we're going?' Chris asked, trying not to sulk. The bronze grumbled but confirmed he could see where they were to go. 'Let's go then.' The sensations of being stretched and compressed at the same time hadn't changed, but for the first time Chris didn't feel queasy. He considered this a huge improvement as the pair appeared above a nearby settlement. With a wave to the rider of the dragon on guard duty he gave Hess the command to take them back to Portum. They reappeared above the pattern of pebbles on the opposite side of the lake to where they'd left Cally and Fin. Cally waved him to come over to her and Hess lazily flapped his wings, landing neatly beside Fin.

'Well?' Cally demanded, 'any better?'

'Yeah, a little,' Chris admitted, taking a swig from his ever-present water bottle.

'Good!' Cally was relieved, 'now, behave yourselves, here come the rest of the group. I want you two to fly over to Escal, over the mountains, you know where it is?'

Chris looked unsure so Cally squatted down and drew a swift map in the sand with a stick.

'What's this bit?' Chris queried.

'That represents the mountains, you cheeky thing.' Cally laughed up at him.

'Ah ok. Got it Hess?' The great bronze head hung over his rider's shoulder before he huffed and the sketch disappeared. 'Come on then, let's stretch your wings.' He leapt to Hess's shoulder with practiced ease and settled himself on his seat pad, tightening the straps and giving Cally a salute before giving Hess the command to take off.

Once they were airborne, Chris could see the rest of the group being called to attention and given their morning schedules. He sighed, he always seemed to be separate from everyone. He'd been separated from his friends when he and Bert left Salutem, now he was separated from Bert as well as his new friends, and even from his classmates. He wondered briefly if he would ever fit in anywhere, then Hess rumbled at him as they rose higher. He slapped the neck of his dragon and they left Portum behind. Hess gave great sweeps of his wings and suddenly they were soaring above the mountains. It was cold up here and Chris was glad of his fur lined leather flying gear. He'd mocked Cally when she'd insisted on getting him some, but this morning he understood.

Sunlight sparkled off Hess's scales as the pair flew across the mountain peaks. They were above the clouds in a magical world where the floor appeared to be white fluff and the sky above them was clear blue. Once over the mountains Chris asked Hess to fly lower so they could navigate to Escal. Flying down through the clouds was cold and wet and by the time they were out again, Chris was wet through, droplets of water streaming from his soaked hair. Shivering, he gave Hess the order to fly straight to Escal, determining privately that they would fly above the clouds all the way back to Portum.

Escal appeared on the horizon, a settlement with tall spires, unusual in this world of dragons and caves. The spires were tall, pointed affairs which Chris could see no use for, but they were certainly individual and would enable him and Hess to get a clear visual easily enough. Hess circled Escal twice as they paid attention to details and formed their personal mental images which would later allow them to jump to Escal if necessary. Cally had told Chris that the Portum dragons took responsibility for defending Escal, where the world leaders resided, and so the imagery was vital to allow the squads to be there as soon as the alarm was raised.

Satisfied that they had the required detail, Chris asked Hess to rise higher again and take them home. They had just broken through the cloud cover when Hess let out a surprised bellow as an image was sent to him by Fin. He showed it to Chris and stunned, Chris gave the order to jump back to Portum.

They arrived above the patterned pebbles moments later to find the bowl in chaos.

A strange golden queen dragon was in the centre of the bowl, guarded on all sides by Portum's own dragons. High on the cliff tops the huge bronze and brown dragons of Portum bellowed their triumph, great spouts of flame issued from them intermittently. The captured queen was calling too, neck stretched to the sky, bellowing at her captors, or for assistance from her fellow wilds, Chris couldn't tell. He urged Hess to move closer and the pair flew across the lake, landing safely out of range of the dragons guarding the newcomer.

Sliding down from his seat, Chris sent Hess back to the lake while he made his way towards the nearest guarding dragon, noting only that it was a green.

'Stay back Midget!'

Looking up, Chris saw Nat astride the green dragon's neck and grinned.

'Only wanting a closer look,' he called back, ducking around the dragon's tail as it swished agitatedly past him.

'We don't know how she'll behave,' Nat called, 'how dangerous she is.'

Now he was closer to the captured queen, Chris wasn't at all sure she was being aggressive, although her behaviour was not that of one of the Portum dragons, she certainly wasn't attempting to attack, or escape. Chris stood for a moment, thinking, wondering if it were possible for him to reach out to a different dragon the way he did with Hess. He tried. Nothing. Instead, he reached for Hess, *'ask her if she's alright.'* Hess, perched on the huge rock at the other side of the lake, stilled as he made contact with the new dragon. Chris waited. *'She is in pain, she needs help.'* The quiet response from Hess worried Chris. He paused, looking at Nat, wondering if he could say what was on his mind to her, recalled that she was never going to be voted rider most likely to stick to the rules and went ahead. 'Nat,' he called, 'come down here a minute, will you?'

Nat frowned down at him. 'Bit busy right now.'

'I know, but...' Chris paused, he didn't want to yell for the whole of Portum to hear. 'Please?'

He saw rather than heard her sigh, but she slipped down the dragon's foreleg, landing next to him. 'What's on your mind, Midget?'

'Listen to her,' Chris said urgently.

Nat frowned, 'Who?' she slapped her green dragon.

'Her.' Chris indicated the trapped queen.

'Not sure I can do that,' Nat looked puzzled.

'Ask your dragon to talk to her.'

Nat leaned against the green flank next to her, absently stroking it as she communicated with her dragon.

Chris watched for the queen's reaction to the contact, saw the huge head lower and cease its restless swaying momentarily, noted the momentary peace as she stopped calling, felt the impact on her. Looking at Nat he saw tears on her cheeks.

'How did you know?' she asked softly.

Chris shrugged, 'I asked Hess to see if she was alright,' he said. 'What can we do?'

'No idea, but here's the man to tell.' She indicated Fallaren, who was striding towards them.

'Nat, why aren't you on Meroden's back, helping?' he snapped.

'Fallaren, wait!' Nat stopped him before he could move on. He turned, anger evident in his blazing eyes. 'She's not dangerous.' Nat said.

Fallaren paused, placing a hand against Meroden as he controlled his emotions. 'I don't know what you're getting at,' he said at last, 'how would you know anything about her? She's a wild dragon.'

'She's in pain.' Chris almost shouted at him, 'I asked Hess to speak to her, he said she's asking for help.'

Fallaren looked at him, shock registering on his face. 'Why would you do that?' he demanded.

'I don't know,' Chris said, 'I tried to reach her myself at first, but I couldn't get through to her, so I asked Hess. There's just something about her. I don't think she's being aggressive.'

Fallaren glanced again at the trapped dragon, then the focus slipped from his eyes as he sought contact with Neldor.

Once again, Chris watched the new queen for her reaction to the angry, powerful man and his bronze. She swung her head around, seeking Neldor, then she called again, but she wasn't challenging.

'I think she's submissive,' Chris said quietly, 'she doesn't want to fight, she wants to join us.'

Fallaren's eyes shot open, he looked at Chris in surprise. 'In all of this,' he waved his hands at the noisy chaos which reigned in the bowl and around the cliffs, 'you chose to reach out to her?'

'I thought she sounded weird,' Chris said, obviously shaken, 'Hess and I got back in the middle of it all, and I just got the feeling she was asking for help, that she wasn't aggressive. I came over here to see if I was right and ran into Nat. But I don't think she's here to cause trouble.' He hoped Fallaren wouldn't think he was crazy, if he did there was nothing Chris could do about it now.

Fallaren was looking closely at Chris, 'Extraordinary,' he said quietly, before turning on his heel and calling for quiet, instructing riders to calm their beasts. Gradually, the noise in the bowl lessened and the dragons on the cliff tops stopped their bellowing.

Chris stood close to Nat, who slung her arm casually around his shoulders, and watched how the strange queen dragon would react to the quiet now surrounding her.

Fallaren approached her, seated on Neldor's neck, he wasn't taking any risks. Chris could see him talking to the huge bronze, watched as the queen settled down into a crouch and wrapped her tail around her, although her head didn't drop for one moment. Slowly, Neldor and Fallaren crept closer to her, tense, ready to attack if she reared up, but she remained in a submissive pose.

Narilka appeared in the bowl. Seeing what Fallaren was doing, her eyes searched the bowl, finding Nat and Chris and quickly trotting towards them.

'Uh-oh, I think we're in trouble now,' Nat whispered.

Chris barely had time to register what was happening before Narilka was upon them.

'What's going on?' she hissed at them. 'What on earth does Fallaren think he's doing? Risking Neldor and possibly the whole of Portum?'

Chris shook his head, 'she's no danger to us, look at her,' he said.

Narilka was looking, watching as the great bronze dragon edged closer and closer. Watching as the new queen hissed at the dragon who was more than twice her size but remained in her crouched position. 'Why did he think this was a good idea?' Narilka said, shaking her head, 'we should be banishing her, send her back to her fellow wilds with the message we don't allow them here.'

Her savage tone surprised Chris, he glanced up at Nat who simply gave his shoulders a brief squeeze. 'Narilka,' he said, his voice shaking, 'I asked Hess to reach out to the queen, she didn't sound right.'

'You stupid boy, of course she didn't sound right,' Narilka snapped, 'she's a wild.'

'No,' Chris said, more firmly this time, 'she wasn't trying to attack, or get away. Hess says she's in pain, she wants to come and join us here.'

Narilka's eyes flicked over him and back to Fallaren and Neldor, who were now right next to the wild queen.

She was calmer now, extending a foreleg, head lowered. He heard Fallaren asking for the Portum dragons to back away, and several dragons took flight, taking up positions in cave mouths. Watchful but a good deal less tense.

As the space around her cleared, the queen sank fully to the ground, crying as she shifted her foreleg around as if attempting to find a comfortable position. A couple of the healers came cautiously towards her, armed with their diagnostic equipment and a basket of supplies. Fallaren and Neldor didn't move as the healers gently examined the leg. After what felt like hours the healers left and the queen appeared peaceful.

Chris reached out to Hess who told him Neldor was trying to encourage her to move to a safe place where she could feed and rest. He turned round to see the young bronze dragon on his perch atop the high rock, he was watching closely as the queen slowly moved in the direction Neldor and Fallaren had asked. Eyes whirling, Hess sought his rider. *She is tired but less afraid now, she will allow the people to look after her, but she has no human to communicate with her, only dragons.*

Chris nodded, watching the queen as she heaved her wings and took off, Neldor hovering above and to one side, guiding her to an empty chamber. She landed awkwardly on the ledge and slowly made her way to the couch. Watching until the very tip of her tail disappeared, Chris turned to Nat and Narilka, 'I wonder if she'll still be here in the morning.'

'Doubt it.' Narilka snapped angrily, 'what a waste of time, she'll be back with her wilds, communicating how easy it is to breach our defences.' She stormed across the bowl towards Neldor and Fallaren, who had left the queen to rest and were now in command in the bowl once more.

Nat let go of Chris and sighed hugely, as if she had been holding her breath through the entire episode. 'Well Midget, you certainly know how to cause trouble, don't you?' Her expression was one of mild approval and Chris grinned at her.

'Didn't mean to cause trouble,' he said, 'but I truly don't think she means us harm, that's not what Hess picked up at all.'

'Hmm, not sure Fallaren is enjoying himself,' Nat said.

Narilka's voice could be heard right across the bowl as she berated her mate. Beside them, Neldor called then lowered his head towards the angry woman, pushing at her, keeping her away from his rider. Everyone saw when Narilka relented, she raised a hand and stroked the bronze muzzle she'd been presented with. Fallaren put his arm around her and together they walked into the cave which housed the healers. Neldor, after a moment's pause, took off in a great cloud of dust and settled on his ledge, basking in the sunshine as if nothing untoward had happened.

'Bit of an anti-climax,' Chris said as around the bowl normal life resumed.

'Yeah, better though,' Nat said, casually vaulting to Meroden's neck, 'let the newbie get used to our normal, see if it suits her. You did good today Squirt, catch ya later.'

Meroden took off, Chris could hear the air creaking as her wings churned the dust around him. Coughing, he put his hand over his mouth and nose until the dust settled. He wasn't sure how he felt about being known as Squirt, Midget was bad enough, but Nat meant no harm and she had said he'd done well. He hoped Fallaren and Narilka agreed.

***

For a few days after the incident with the appearance of the wild queen, all training flights were cancelled, and no dragons left the bowl unless it was deemed essential. It seemed the whole of Portum was waiting, holding its collective breath to see how the situation would play out.

Finally, on the fourth day after her arrival, the new queen left her new lodgings to fly to the lake where she went for a swim. The empty bowl filled as word got around what was happening, and silent crowds watched the glittering dragon as she wallowed in the deep, cool water. The healers who had been caring for her came galloping across the bowl with fresh dressings and potions for her. They sat on the rocks and waited for her to emerge from the water.

Among the crowds, Anilla and Jay found Chris and the three friends watched as the golden dragon slowly left the water. She shook herself and flipped her wings to her back before extending her leg towards the healers and allowing them to tend to her wounds. Once they had finished applying fresh dressings, she took off again and went straight back to her quarters, landing neatly on the ledge before settling down to sun herself. She observed the bowl, great eyes whirling and glittering in the sunlight.

'Well,' Jay said at last, 'looks like she's setting in nicely.' He gave a nervous laugh.

'How will she cope here with no rider?' Anilla said, 'I've heard they're having trouble communicating with her, only a small number of dragons can make her understand them, it's like she speaks a different dragon language to the Portum dragons.'

'Seems likely,' Chris said, 'when that last attack happened, when the black dragon was badly wounded, Hess said he could hear strange dragons but couldn't understand them.'

'I suppose it's like us coming from the caves into Portum.' Jay said thoughtfully, 'the language is a bit different, and we didn't always understand what folk were saying to us at first.'

'Still not sure about Garad and Edwin sometimes,' Chris laughed.

'Will she be allowed to stay here?' Jay wondered, 'I mean, if she's riderless. Won't that be a problem next time there's an attack?'

'I don't know,' Anilla sighed, 'I'm sure they'll come up with something, some way to keep her safe if she chooses to stay, but so far, I have no idea what the plan is, if indeed there is one.'

'What about Remnac's brother?' Chris said hesitantly. 'I mean, would it even be possible?'

'Would what be possible?' Anilla asked.

'Could he have another dragon?' Chris said, following his thoughts slowly. 'His dragon died after that great black brute scorched him, I was thinking he, or another rider whose dragon died, might be able to take her on?'

'Don't be silly,' Anilla snapped, 'no man has ever ridden a queen dragon.' She paused, 'and I don't think there's ever been a case of a rider getting a second chance of a dragon either.'

'Does that mean it can't ever happen though?' Jay asked, 'It would make sense, to me at least, if someone with experience could pair up with her. You get to know body language and so on, even if the normal means of communication isn't possible.'

Anilla shrugged, 'I doubt it will be considered,' she said.

Chris sighed, reluctantly dragging his gaze from the wild queen dragon. He wondered if she knew he and Hess were the ones who had made that first contact with her. Shrugging, he returned to the classroom and Remnac.

***

The following day Chris made his way to the classroom after lunch for what he hoped would be an interesting afternoon with Remnac and the rest of his class. However, when he entered the classroom, Remnac called him to the front and made him stand next to him. As the rest of the class assembled, many curious glances were cast in his direction. Chris felt himself grow hot and hoped he wasn't blushing as he stood there beside Remnac. Once everyone was seated, Remnac cleared his throat.

'Good afternoon class,' he began, 'I have an

announcement to make. Chris here will not be joining us for lessons anymore.'

Chris's head whipped around to look at Remnac. 'Why?' he demanded, fearing the worst.

'Because you've passed all the lessons I have to teach you lad. You're going to graduate to your permanent wing today, and tomorrow you'll be given your schedule so you can return to work part time.'

Chris was delighted, the rest of the faces in the room looked less than happy.

'Someone from your new squad will be along shortly to tell you where you've been placed,' Remnac continued, 'and then, after you've met your new team, you'll be expected to go to your workplace and arrange your schedule with them. Alright?'

'Alright? It's brilliant!' Chris could hardly keep still.

Remnac laughed at him, 'Go take a seat while we wait for whoever it is.'

'Don't you know?' Ranya demanded, infuriated when Remnac shrugged and grinned at her.

Chris took his usual seat next to Tom, who thumped his arm and said 'Congratulations,' in a stage whisper.

'Thanks.' Chris said, dragging his eyes away from the door.

Ten minutes later, when no one had appeared, he was forced to pay attention to what Remnac was saying to the class about their own graduations. He was giving a run through of where everyone else was when the door finally opened.

Chris turned and saw Nat strolling into the room. She grinned at him.

'Hey Midget, welcome to Osprey,' she called, 'come on, the guys are waiting to meet you.'

Chris was on his feet before she'd finished speaking. He turned at the door and gave a brief wave to the rest of the group before walking away with Nat.

CHAPTER 17

Chris followed Nat down the passageway to the outside world, breathing a huge sigh of relief as they made it out into the warm sunshine. Nat paused, turning to look at him.

'You alright there?' she asked, 'Ready for the real world?'

'Yep,' Chris said, he could hardly believe his luck.

'Good lad,' Nat reached out to ruffle his hair, thought better of it and gripped his shoulder instead. 'Come on, I've told them all about you and that bronze monster of yours,' she grinned at his hiss of protest.

Nat led the way to a set of steps which had been hewn into the wall of the bowl and began climbing.

'Wouldn't it be easier to fly?' Chris asked as he panted behind her.

'Yeah, but you and Hess don't have your accommodation assigned yet, and it's not a good idea to land a strange dragon on another dragon's ledge.' Nat told him.

'Fair enough I suppose,' Chris was struggling to keep up with her long legs.

Nat glanced back over her shoulder and slowed her

pace a little. 'Sorry Midget,' she said, 'I forgot you're not used to this yet.'

Chris glared at her, grateful for the easing of pace. 'How much higher are we going?' He asked, looking down and instantly regretting it.

'Not far now,' Nat said cheerfully.

Chris edged as far as he could to the inner wall as they continued to climb. Finally, Nat stopped at a large cave entrance. Chris could hear voices inside and suddenly nerves flared in his stomach.

'You'll be fine,' Nat said, unexpectedly reassuring him, 'the rest of the squad can't wait to meet you. Come on, get it over with.' She stepped from the stairway and into the mouth of the cave.

'Nat! At last, you've been ages. Well, where is he?' An impatient male voice said.

Chris gulped, took a deep breath and followed her into the cave entrance. A group of riders were all looking at him in silence. He felt his heart racing and for one awful moment he thought he was about to faint, but Nat grabbed his arm and pulled him into the cave, which turned out to be the Osprey meeting room.

'Here you are Midget, meet your new team,' Nat held fast to his arm as she made introductions. 'This is Brent, he's squad leader.'

Brent wasn't much taller than Nat, a powerfully built man, his dark hair flopped over his face, he shook it back and extended a hand to Chris, 'Welcome to Osprey young man,' he said in the deepest voice Chris had ever heard.

'Thanks,' Chris replied, shaking Brent's hand. Annoyingly, nerves made his own voice barely more than a whisper.

'This is Jimmy,' Nat indicated a rider towards the back of the group. He was incredibly tall and thin, 'he's our squad second,' Nat continued as Jimmy nodded his welcome at Chris.

One by one Nat introduced the Ospreys, 'This is Nate, Lan, Sol, Will, Alice, but don't call her that, she's likely to kill you, we call her Ice...' Chris felt his head starting to spin, he was certain he'd never remember all these names. Then Nat came to Dar and Jake.

To his surprise, Dar gripped him warmly by both shoulders. 'Welcome,' he said, 'you'll be fine here, we'll all help you settle in.'

'Yeah, must be a lot to take in,' Jake added, slapping Chris on the back, 'glad you're with us kiddo.'

Chris began to feel a little better and was able to return Jake's smile.

'Right, accommodation assignment,' Brent said, suddenly business-like. 'You and Hess will be in J12. Nat, can you show him where that is please?' Nat nodded. 'Now,' Brent was addressing Chris again, 'I know you've just been through training with Rem and Cally, but your real rider training is just about to start.' Brent continued, 'you'll fly with us a few times in training sessions, but you're also going to need individual training to get you and your dragon up to standard. Alright?'

It was clear that he had no choice in the matter, but Chris nodded anyway. At least Remnac had warned them all about this extra training period. 'Training starts tomorrow?' he asked.

'You're keen!' Jimmy laughed.

Brent chuckled, 'No, I think we'll give you time to settle into your new quarters first. I'll sort out the squad training schedule, it's due an overhaul, then you can sort out your work schedule with your craft before you start with us.'

'He's always like this,' Nat said, 'Rem says he's powered through his lessons, both in the classroom and the flying with Cally. She can't fault him, by the way, says the only trouble might be Hess being a bit headstrong.'

Chris snorted at this. 'A bit?'

'Yeah, I hear he's like his rider,' Dar said.

'Well, you know, I like to get on with things,' Chris said, grinning at Dar, 'so I work hard. Hess is the same, we get bored easily, so we push ourselves.'

Nat was grinning at him, 'Midget, you're going to show us all up,' she laughed, 'come on, let me show you where you're going to be living. It's much better than the cupboard Rem shoved you in. Hess will love all the space he's getting, he might grow even bigger, and I know how much you love sanding dragon hide.'

There was a chorus of laughter as Chris followed Nat from the cave, only to find his way blocked by a large, green shape. Meroden had come to give them a lift.

'Climb aboard,' Nat said cheerily, vaulting gracefully to her seat at the base of Meroden's neck. Chris scrambled up behind her. He hardly had time to make himself secure before Meroden was gliding around the bowl. Nat turned around to speak to Chris. 'You see where we've just been?' she shouted above the wind whistling round their ears, pointing to the huge cave mouth where he could just see Dar and Jake watching them and waving. Chris waved back and nodded at Nat.

Meroden glided idly down to the floor of the bowl and settled herself comfortably as her rider and Chris dismounted. Nat stood next to the huge head, using it as a prop as she leaned back a little and looked up at the cliff face. 'Right Midget,' she said, 'you see how the ledges of the caves have coloured markers on them?'

Chris squinted up at the cave mouths, noticing for the first time the coloured paint on each side of the openings. 'I never saw that before,' he said.

'Not many folk do,' Nat said, 'but it makes it easier to recognise the different squad areas. I'll take you and Hess to your quarters in a minute, yours is…' she paused, moving her finger along as she counted in her head. 'Third level down, two to the right of the meeting cave.'

'Ok,' he said, 'should I call Hess to me?'

'Nah, Merry and I will take you up there first, so you can look around, then we'll go find the bronze one,' she laughed.

They mounted Meroden once more and she took off from the bowl, she was much quicker into the air than Hess and Chris found himself clinging onto the straps for dear life. Before he knew it, they were landing on the ledge of his new home. He slid down Merry's foreleg and surveyed his new territory.

The first area was for Hess, and it was enormous. The raised area for the dragon's bed was double the size of the one Hess was currently squeezing himself onto.

Plenty of space for a growing dragon. Chris nodded his approval. 'Hess is going to love this,' he said to Nat, who was lounging on the ledge with Merry.

'Wait until he discovers it echoes in here,' she said, 'you'll get sick of hearing him bellow, until he gets tired of it himself.'

'Wonderful,' Chris said, 'hope he lets me sleep. Speaking of which…' He turned to his right and entered his own accommodation. It was all a bit basic with bare floor and walls and he had an unpleasant moment as memories of Salutem rose in his mind. However, the space was large, with a big bed in one corner, the mattress piled high with blankets and a couple of furs. There was a fireplace, a couple of wooden chairs, a table and a couch. A strange looking tube hung next to the fireplace, with a keypad next to it. Chris stared at it for a moment, wondering what it could be, making up his mind to ask Nat when he'd finished looking around.

To the left of the fireplace was another opening, this one curtained, he wandered over and peeped into the next room. It was his very own bathing room, with a big double tub and some rustic looking plumbing, Chris smirked when he saw it, wondering if he and Bert could improve upon it. There was a stone sink set on a wooden bench with a large pottery jug standing in it. The other necessary facilities were hidden away behind a curtain in the corner. All in all, he decided he was happy with his new home. He would make it cosier over time with rugs and wall hangings, and a curtain between himself and Hess. He had a feeling that the young bronze would try to join him in his bed if he could squeeze through the open archway.

He made his way back to Nat and Meroden, who were happily sunning themselves on his ledge. He put a hand to the grey paint on the side of the cave mouth, the number of his home was painted over the grey in solid black lettering. He traced the J12 with his fingertips, revelling in the idea that this was his home now. There was hard work ahead of him, he knew that, but it was worth it.

'Ready?' Nat said quietly behind him.

He turned and nodded at her, 'Yes, let's go get Hess,' he said. Then a thought struck him, 'will he need much practice at landing on the ledge?' he asked, suddenly worried that he might fall off, or Hess might be injured.

'Oh, you'll be surprised how quickly they get used to it,' Nat assured him, 'and from what I've heard he's an agile little fella.'

'Not so little anymore,' Chris said with feeling, 'he's already outgrown our student accommodation really.'

'Come on then, let's go get the lad, let him enjoy his new vantage point.' Nat helped Chris up onto Meroden's shoulder before leaping confidently up herself. 'Always a little tricky doing this on a ledge,' she said over her shoulder, 'but you'll soon get used to it. Dar can come down his tunnel at a full run and vault onto Triant's neck, Jake does it too, and a few of the others. I think it's a boy thing myself, Nell and I have never seen the need.'

Meroden almost fell from the ledge, gliding lazily across to the lake where Hess sat, sunning himself on the big rock while he watched Cally putting the other dragons through their paces.

'Nat,' Chris almost had to shout to be heard over

the rushing air, 'what's that tube thing near the fireplace?'

'Speaking tube,' Nat yelled back, 'I'll show you how it all works later.'

Satisfied, Chris concentrated on keeping his seat as Meroden whirled around the lake before landing next to Hess.

'Show off,' Nat said, giving the green an affectionate thump.

Chris dismounted, hoping he wouldn't make a fool of himself with the rest of his class looking on. Then he reminded himself that he wasn't part of the class anymore. He felt sadness wash over him. Would he always be an outsider? Would he ever fit into Osprey the way Nat, Dar and everyone else had? He landed heavily, but managed to stay on his feet, hoping he made it look easier than it was as he leaned against Meroden for a moment, stroking her neck to cover his need to stand still for a moment. Then he looked up at Hess, who was watching him with interest.

'Come on, you great lump, let's go get you settled into your new home.' He called up to him.

Hess rose, eyes whirling with interest, and half jumped, half glided down to his rider. He looked at Meroden, who gazed back, then Nat laughed. 'Merry says Hess doesn't like you stroking her,' she relayed to Chris.

Chris laughed, 'Get used to Merry,' he said to the bronze, 'we're part of the same team now. Come on, let me get up on your neck and let's go see where we live now.' He clambered up the leg Hess extended and settled himself. Meroden leapt skywards, Hess followed close behind her and Chris guided him towards their ledge.

Hess flew straight towards their new home, back winging at the last minute to land neatly. Seeing his new sleeping arrangements, he trundled towards his new couch without allowing Chris to dismount.

'Hey!' Chris thumped the bronze shoulder beneath him, 'let me off first you great lump!' He heard laughter behind him and turned to see Merry had landed on the ledge.

Hess paused for long enough to allow Chris to slide down from his perch before he settled himself on his new couch, humming happily to himself. Chris stood watching him in disbelief as Nat walked up behind him and put a hand on his shoulder.

'He looks happy,' she said, 'let's hope you settle in just as well.'

'Hope so,' Chris said with a small sigh, glancing through the doorway into the bare apartment which was his.

'Let me show you how the tube works,' Nat said, 'then I'll take you down to stores and we can get you some rugs and stuff, make the place look more like home.' She ruffled his hair and wandered into the main room. 'I forgot how huge these places look with nothing in them,' she said, walking across to the fireplace. 'Right Midget, come over here.' Chris wandered over to her. Nat picked up the end of the tube and stood to one side a little so Chris could see the keypad next to it. 'This,' she waved the tube under his nose, 'is a communication device. The numbers on the pad all relate to different people or places. For instance,' she pressed the two followed immediately by the five. Almost immediately a gruff male voice said

'What?' 'Only me,' Nat said cheerfully, 'just showing Chris how this thing works.'

'Who was that?' Chris asked.

'Jake,' she told him, 'He's always grumpy when he has to use the tube, prefers to talk face to face.'

'How will I know the numbers for everyone?' Chris asked, sure he would never get the hang of this contraption.

'There should be a list somewhere,' Nat said, looking around. When it became obvious there was no list she picked up the tube again and dialled eleven. A female voice answered immediately. 'Soph, it's Nat, I'm just showing our new lad how the tube works, and he doesn't have the list of numbers. He's in J12, could you make sure one appears for him please?' Once she'd received an affirmative response, Nat let the tube dangle from its hook in the wall.

'Is she in Osprey too?' he asked, certain he'd not heard the name before.

'No, she works down with Rem, keeps all the paperwork straight. At least, she tries. She's nice.' Nat told him.

'I'll never be able to use that thing,' Chris said, 'I mean, why would anyone want to hear from me?'

'Brent or Jimmy will use it to contact you about meetings, schedules and so on.' Nat said, 'and you'll soon find yourself getting over it when you want food. The number for the kitchens is the one most of us memorise first.' She laughed, shaking her short curls. 'Right, let's leave Hess to his comfy new bed, Merry and I will take you to the stores for some bits to make this place your home.' She urged him back into the tunnel and past a now sleeping Hess. Once they were seated safely on Merry's neck, Nat gave the order to leave and Merry dropped into a glide down to the huge caves at the base of the cliffs.

Nat led the way into the first cave mouth and Chris, following her, stopped short in shock. The walls of the cave were fitted with shelves which stretched high above his head, as far back as he could see, and the cave was enormous. Boxes were stacked around the floor and, to his left, was a great table piled high with more boxes and stacks of plates and mugs.

'Welcome to Portum stores,' Nat said, grinning at his surprise. 'Let's get started, shall we?'

'I don't even know where to start,' Chris said faintly.

'It's ok Midget, I do!' Nat set off, whistling between her teeth, heading towards the nearest shelving. 'You need rugs,' she said firmly, 'cos those floors get cold, even in the summer.' She indicated a stack of rolled rugs, 'what sort of colours do you like?'

Chris had no idea, 'Um, anything really,' he said, 'but not pink,' he added hurriedly.

Nat nodded and pulled a couple from the stack for him to inspect.

Once the rugs were selected they wandered further into the cave and added wall hangings to the pile, followed by heavy woollen throws and some pillows and a couple of huge floor cushions, which Nat insisted were perfect for curling up on in front of the fire. They were soon joined by plates, mugs, cutlery, a couple of bowls, candles, a water jug, and some glasses. Then Nat dragged him right to the back of the cave and showed him the racks of clothing.

'We need to get you some flying gear,' she said, holding up a thickly lined jacket against him. 'Try this on for size.'

'I already have flying gear,' Chris protested.

'You'll need more than one set.' Nat said firmly, 'plus Brent and Jimmy will be arranging for your squad jacket, makes it easier to see who's in which team when we're flying for real.'

Reluctantly, Chris obeyed, slipping his arms into the jacket she was holding. The jacket was big enough to fit Jay in there with him. He laughed, flapping his arms so the too long sleeves waved around. Nat selected another jacket for him to try, and on the third attempt she found the perfect fit for him. Next came the trousers, helmet, and a pair of sturdy boots, some socks and other clothing.

He was beginning to wonder how all of this would make it up to his home near the top of the cliffs when a man appeared. 'What's going on?' he demanded.

'Hey Austin,' Nat said, 'sorting young Chris out, he's just joined Osprey and his room's a bit on the bare side.'

'Ah, I've heard about you,' Austin said, looking at Chris with interest. He held out his hand, 'Austin, pleased to meet you. I take it Nat has shown you where everything is? If there's anything else you need, just come find me, I'll do my best to get you sorted.'

Chris stammered his thanks before Austin turned and left them to it.

'OK Midget?' Nat asked, 'anything else you can think of?'

'I didn't think of any of this,' Chris pointed out, 'but no, thank you, I can't think of anything else right now.'

'Goodo,' Nat's bubbly personality was starting to make him feel tired, and it wasn't even lunchtime yet. 'Let's take all this to the front and Austin will take it from there. He needs to cross things off his lists.'

Together they carried the pile of clothing and added it to the heaped household goods they had selected earlier.

Austin appeared beside them. 'He's in J12,' Nat told him.

'No worries,' Austin said, 'I'll arrange delivery.'

Chris had assumed they would be asking Merry and Hess to transport the goods, but Austin had other ideas. He thanked him and followed Nat back out into the sunshine.

'What next?' he asked her.

'Well now, you need to go see your craft master,' she said, 'and plan for returning to work. But first you'll need your squad schedule, so I guess we'd better go see Brent and Jimmy, see if they've got it sorted out yet. C'mon.' She leapt up onto Meroden's shoulder, leaning down to drag Chris up behind her. Moments later Merry was airborne and heading for the meeting cave he'd seen this morning.

Merry dropped them off then disappeared to her own ledge, leaving the cave entrance free for other dragons of the squad should they need it. Some of the Osprey members had left, but still Brent and Jimmy were surrounded by half a dozen riders, all arguing about something.

'Hey guys,' Nat called, 'got those schedules sorted out yet? Chris needs to go sort out his work rota.'

'Does it sound like we've got it sorted?' Brent glared at her, 'be easier if I didn't have to listen to this lot.' He indicated the men surrounding him.

'Ah, I have time to give you a haircut then Midget,' Nat said cheerfully, tugging on Chris's locks, which were reaching for his shoulders, 'looks like you're well overdue one.'

Chris was about to open his mouth when several male voices yelled 'NO!' Stunned, he looked at the other riders.

One man, whom he didn't recall seeing earlier, stepped forward. He was built like the master smith, tall with huge, muscular shoulders and arms. 'Don't let her anywhere near your hair lad,' he said, 'Brent let her cut his hair once, he's still trying to grow it out.' He grinned suddenly, showing white teeth, his eyes crinkled and twinkled down at Chris. 'I'm Ty,' he held out his hand, 'I didn't make it to the meet and greet earlier. Pleased to see you're in Osprey though, heard a lot about you.'

'Thanks,' Chris said, shaking his hand as firmly as he could, while behind him Nat sighed dramatically.

'I don't know what your problem is,' she said, 'you all need haircuts and I'm offering to help you all out.'

'We'd rather be bald.' Ty said, winking at Chris before returning to the table where Brent and Jimmy were wrestling with the schedule.

'Will there be regular times for training then?' Chris asked, wandering over to the group. He was feeling a little more confident now that everyone seemed friendly towards him. It was a nice change.

'That is what I'm trying to work out.' Brent huffed, 'but fitting everyone's work in with the training is proving traumatic.'

'Won't the crafts work around training then?' Chris asked reasonably.

'Yes,' Brent said, glowering at Ty and Jimmy, 'but some of the riders won't!'

'Ah.' Chris looked down at the charts scattered over the large table. They didn't make much sense to him, covered in scrawl and symbols he didn't understand. 'I'll nip over to see Garad and Edwin shall I? See when's best for me to be at work?'

Jimmy and Ty burst into loud laughter; Brent sagged onto the table. 'Yeah, you do that kid,' he said, 'make my job harder.'

Nat wandered over and handed Chris a mug of batu. 'Usually, we train in the early mornings or late afternoon,' she told him, 'Don't understand where the problem is.'

'The problem,' Brent said in a tight voice, 'is Ty insisting that he needs to work full days for a while.'

'How long a while?' Nat asked.

'Only a couple of weeks,' Ty said quickly, 'we're finishing up a big project and they need everyone on board.'

'Well, you said you wanted to give Hess and I time

to settle in before training starts,' Chris pointed out, 'That gives me time to get back into things with Garad and Edwin, and gives Hess time to settle in.'

Nat snorted, 'He's already settled in,' she said, 'Fast asleep in his bed,' she told the others.

Brent straightened up from the table, 'You sure?' he asked Chris, 'I don't want you to feel we're not taking you and Hess seriously, but it'd really take the pressure off. Nate, Jimmy and I can take you on training flights initially then, get you used to flying with others around you.'

'I don't mind, I understand the situation, and to be perfectly honest I'd like time to get to know you all before I start flying with everyone and learning how Osprey works in the air. Training with the three of you sounds way less intimidating,' he gave a half laugh, hoping it didn't betray his nerves.

Jimmy, Ty and Dar were nodding, Nat slung an arm around Chris's shoulders and gave him a squeeze. 'Well said Midget,' she said quietly.

'Well, if you're sure,' Brent said gratefully, 'it would be a big help.'

'I'm sure,' Chris said simply, 'I'll nip and give Garad and Edwin the good news, I'm sure they'll be delighted to meet Hess. If I can wake him up.' He left the meeting cave and trotted up the external steps to his new home.

Hess lifted his head as Chris walked towards him, blinking at his friend. 'Come on lazybones, we're going visiting.' Chris said cheerfully, grabbing the harness which he hadn't had time to remove and giving it a tug. Slowly, the bronze dragon rose to his feet and trundled towards the edge of his new ledge. Chris carefully climbed to his seat at the base of his neck and tightened the straps. 'This'll be a nice place for you to sunbathe,' he told Hess, 'Come on, let's go make you some new friends.'

Hess fell off the ledge and glided for a moment before his wings began working, lifting them higher, above the cliffs. Then they flew in a leisurely fashion over Portum, circling around the huge area before coming to land outside the paper crafting building.

Chris had barely had chance to slide down along Hess's foreleg when the door flew open and Garad's face appeared.

'Ed,' he called back into the room, 'Come see who's here.'

Before Chris could take a step both paper makers were beside him, although he noted they kept a wary eye on Hess, who was looking at these new people with interest. He extended his head towards Edwin, sniffing him and flicking his tongue out at him.

Edwin froze, Chris laughed. 'Hess, behave yourself,' he said, 'these are my friends, be nice to them.' Hess rumbled, but settled himself down, tail curling around his legs. 'Will you let them stroke you?' he asked. Hess turned huge eyes on his rider before lowering his chin to the floor with a huff.

'You can stroke him,' Chris told Garad, who reached cautiously towards the bronze head.

'He's so soft and smooth,' Garad said softly, 'You're quite the handsome lad, aren't you?'

Hess rustled his wings and Chris felt a wave of

approval from him for Garad. He laughed, 'He likes you,' he told Garad, who began stroking a little more confidently.

Edwin hung back, 'What are you doing here?' he asked Chris.

'We've graduated to our squad now,' Chris told him, 'So I'm here to work out my schedule with you guys. I can come back to work.'

'Marvellous!' Edwin said, 'we've missed you, and now that young Jay's got himself a dragon too, we're all on our own again and we've got used to you two young 'uns being around.'

Garad reluctantly dragged his attention away from Hess. 'Come inside,' he said, 'let's see what we can work out.'

'Hess, you stay here and be good,' Chris said, watching as the dragon settled himself happily in the sunshine. 'We'll hear him snoring soon I expect,' he said as he turned to follow Garad and Edwin indoors.

CHAPTER 18

The next two weeks were joyous for Chris. He worked with Garad and Edwin each morning and undertook individual training sessions in the afternoons with Brent, Jimmy and Nate.

The only problem was Hess, who wanted to be wherever his rider was. Despite all Chris's efforts to persuade him to go back to his new home ledge, the paper crafters found themselves with a new bronze mascot. Whenever Chris was at work Hess could be found curled up near the doorway, happily snoozing while he waited for his friend.

'What are we going to do when Jay comes back?' Chris asked Garad, 'If Sorbus wants to copy Hess you might have two of them out there.'

'Fine by me,' Garad said, 'I like having him out there, and he's no trouble.'

'First time for everything,' Chris muttered under his breath before returning his attention to the soaking wood pulp he was heaving into frames to dry.

***

The afternoon training sessions were fun and exhausting in equal parts. Although Hess did most of the hard work, Chris found himself struggling to keep up with the demands of the older riders. Hess however loved it, he enjoyed keeping up with the bigger bronze dragons, even Nate's brown Ata was bigger than he was, and Hess saw it as a challenge to keep up.

Chris was thankful the bathing routine was simpler now, and Hess was capable of catching his own food from the herds penned for that purpose. His first few forays had ended in disappointment for him, so he'd taken it upon himself to perch on the fence and watch while Brent's bronze Golian and Ice's silver Farlie had caught their meals. After that he'd had no issues, although the feeding herd had required replenishing more often.

Now his evenings were full of friendship as he settled in with his squad and got to know everyone. He was rapidly becoming firm friends with Nat, Dar and Jake, but Ice, Ty, Nate and Nell often joined them in the meeting cave for card games.

**

Chris had been a full member of Osprey for two weeks when Ty announced that the big project the smiths had been working on was completed and he was now available for the full training schedule.

'What was the project?' Chris asked Ty, 'can you tell us now that it's all done?'

'Yeah,' Ty shrugged, 'we've been working on the hydroelectric thing, bringing running water to Portum.' He grinned, 'Your mate was helping too, Bertie isn't it? He's full of himself, glad you're not like that Midget.'

Chris grimaced, most of the squad had heard Nat's nickname for him and copied it. 'Bert's alright,' he countered, 'haven't seen him for ages though.'

'He's coming up to the dragon bowl tomorrow,' Ty told him, 'Fetching a load of pipes up, ready for the water to be connected here too.'

'Oh! I might nip down and see him then,' Chris said, wondering how Bert would react to being so close to the hundreds of Portum dragons. 'If we're not busy that is,' he glanced over to the table where once again Brent had the charts out, attempting to arrange full squad training that would suit everyone's schedules.

The rest of Osprey were sitting around, drinking batu and chatting. Ice, the temperamental rider of silver Farlie, was giving Nate her opinion on something. He didn't look like he was enjoying the experience.

Chris was sitting with Dar, Jake and Ty talking about training and how he and Hess were doing.

'He's game, I'll give you that much,' Dar said, 'don't like being left behind, does he?'

Chris laughed, 'Hess works hard,' he countered, 'he wants to be a grown-up dragon, like Triant.'

'Ah, but Tri's only a blue,' Ty said, teasing Dar, 'you should have seen him straining to keep up with my Ata. He did it though,' he admitted, 'he's determined.'

Chris nodded, 'He likes Ata,' he told Ty, 'Likes the competition, as he sees it.'

'Just as long as he doesn't overdo things,' Jake said, 'we've had it before, haven't we? Young blue wanted to boss it over the bronzes, got badly hurt in the process. We almost lost him.'

'Oh! That's terrible,' Chris cried. 'Is he still in the

squad?' he asked, running through the blue dragons in Osprey in his mind.

'Nah, they shunted him and his rider out to one of the small villages to run messages.' Jake said, 'keep him out of trouble, makes himself useful and there's no competition so he's not pushing himself too much.'

'Right guys.' Brent's voice lifted above the chatter of the Osprey riders, 'I have our new schedule here.' He waved a large piece of hide above his head. 'I've tried to include everyone's work schedules, but I'm afraid some of you will need to have talks with your craft masters. They need to understand that the dragons come first.' He wandered to the large noticeboard and tacked up the schedule.

Immediately a few of the riders went to look and voices were raised in complaint. Brent retreated to the table and began tidying up the hides and papers which he and Jimmy had scattered around.

'I did warn you,' he said to the riders who were complaining, 'but we need a regular schedule, especially as we have a new member, and at least one more joining us shortly.'

'Who's coming up to Osprey?' Nat called to him.

'Not sure yet, but it looks like we might be getting a second queen.'

All eyes swivelled to Ice, who had stopped berating Nate and was now scowling at Brent.

'I know nothing for sure yet,' Brent told her, 'But it's likely we'll get another queen, most of the other squads have a couple. Farlie won't mind I daresay...' he let his voice trail off.

Ice simply shrugged and drank her batu.

'I hope they're not going to send Ranya and Tathdel to us,' Chris said quietly, 'I can't see her fitting in here at all.'

'I think they're already assigned to a squad,' Dar told him, 'Pretty sure I saw them in Curlew.'

'Good!' Chris said, more forcefully than he'd intended.

'Nah, looks like we might be getting a blue and a brown from your group, and possibly a brown and a queen from elsewhere,' Brent told them, sauntering over with a mug of batu. He sat down next to Jake with a sigh. 'I wish they'd all remember that we're riders first,' he said.

'They'll get over it,' Dar said, 'it's always like this, you can't please everybody, so you need to do what's best for the squad.'

There were nods all round and Brent raised his mug to them before draining the contents.

'Brent!' Jimmy's voice was urgent. 'don't forget we need to...'

'Ah! Yes,' Brent stood up and strolled towards the back of the cave, where Jimmy was standing. There was a strange rustling noise which made Chris look over to see what was going on, but it was dark back there and he couldn't make out what they were up to.

'Wonder who we're getting from my class,' he said, mentally running through the dragon colours and matching them with riders. 'Hope we get Tom; he's got a brown and he's a nice lad. There were a few blues, Tate's the best of the bunch there.'

Dar shrugged, 'we'll find out soon enough,' he said, 'if they have rough corners we'll soon knock them off for them.'

'Chris, could you come here for a moment please,' Brent called, he was holding something in his hands.

Chris rose and went to him, aware as he did so that the rest of the squad were watching.

'I'd just like to say how pleased we all are that you've been put in Osprey with us.' Brent said, 'I need to give you this. You're one of us now.' He handed Chris a fur lined jacket which he'd folded turned inside out.

'Thanks,' Chris said, taking it from him and giving it a shake. As the garment turned the right way out he saw the grey of the sleeves and the symbol on the collar. He turned it round to look at the back, where a large shield of grey held the silhouette of an Osprey. He looked back at Brent, eyes shining. 'Thank you.' Annoyingly his voice wavered, and he felt tears stinging his eyes. Finally, he belonged.

CHAPTER 19

The following day dawned with heavy cloud cover and rain falling over Portum. When Chris peered out of the doorway he saw grey, misty rain sleeting down. No dragons were in evidence except for the wild golden queen, who sat on her ledge looking around, occasionally shaking water droplets from her head.

The Portum dragons were still having a hard time communicating with her and she was refusing most attempts to persuade her to settle down. Hess managed to understand her, but he told Chris that she spoke differently to the dragons here, so he used images when he was near her, to show her. Still, there was little anyone could do with her, and she was widely regarded as dangerous.

Chris returned to his living quarters, licked his lips nervously and picked up the speaking tube. He glanced at the list Soph had provided for him, took a deep breath and pressed in the number for the kitchens. Almost immediately a female voice spoke.

'Yes?'

'Erm, um, please could you send me some breakfast up?' Chris asked, his eyes screwed up tight.

The expected rebuff didn't arrive. Instead, the woman said, 'Room number?'

'Oh, er, I'm in J12.' Chris replied, stunned.

'It'll be with you as soon as we can.' The woman cut the connection and Chris replaced the tube in its holder, a dazed expression on his face.

'This is going to take some getting used to,' he said quietly.

He wandered around his accommodation; the novelty still hadn't worn off that this space was all his. He tweaked the rugs, his rugs he corrected himself, and straightened the cushions on the couch. He was about to go look at Hess when a rumbling sound beneath his feet shook him. Panicking, he held onto the back of a chair, certain that this must be one of those quake things Anilla had told him about.

The rumbling stopped abruptly and beside the fireplace a hatch flew open, revealing his breakfast. Stunned, Chris walked across the room and lifted the tray out of the opening. He stuck his head inside what turned out to be a box of sorts. Bemused, he took his breakfast over to the table and removed the covers from the dishes. Seating himself with a happy sigh he began his attack on the plate full of bacon, eggs and sausages. He also had a jug of batu all to himself and a couple of pieces of fruit. Heaven!

Once he'd finished his meal, saving the fruit for later, he placed the tray back into the box and closed the hatch. Immediately the rumbling began again. After a few moments he opened the hatch to see a stone shaft with a heavy chain hanging down the centre of the space. 'Ingenious,' he said, reaching in and giving the chain an experimental pull.

Closing the hatch, he wandered out to see Hess, who was awake now and demanding his own breakfast. Chris grabbed the harness and soon the pair were gliding across the bowl towards the feeding pens. Chris slid from his seat and immediately Hess launched himself towards the herd.

Leaning against the fence, Chris became aware of strange noises coming along the rough road towards the dragon bowl. Clanging and clanking and raised voices heralded the arrival of the smiths. He saw Bert among them, pushing a large cart piled high with metal tubes which were held in place by several stout logs, lashed to the sides of the cart in an upright position. As the cart bumped and bounced over the ruts and stones in the road, the tubes kept shifting, making an unholy racket.

Glancing around the bowl Chris saw dragon and human heads peeking out to see what the commotion was about. He looked over at Hess, who was happily eating his breakfast and paying no attention to the antics of the humans. Chris climbed onto the top rail of the fence and perched there, clinging to a post for stability, watching the strange procession as it entered the bowl and made its way to the huge caverns which housed the kitchens.

A few dragons were showing interest in the goings on now, and riders and kitchen staff were converging on the smiths, demanding to know what was going on. Chris saw Ty emerging from the kitchens, heard his loud voice issuing orders, growing louder as he was ignored. Grinning, Chris called Hess to test his readiness to stop eating. Almost immediately Hess was with him. Chris swung off the fence directly onto the seat pad at the base of the bronze neck and asked Hess to take them both to the bowl. 'There's someone I want you to meet,' Chris said.

Hess landed as close to the kitchens as he could but was shooed away by Ty and the other smiths. 'Sorry Midget, not now,' Ty called to him, 'we gotta get this lot under cover as soon as we can.'

Chris shrugged and raised his hand in acknowledgment of Ty's instruction, ordering Hess to move away. Hess took him to the centre of the bowl where they could watch what was happening but not be in the way. He saw Bert watching him and waved cheerily, Bert nodded back at him but was busy trying not to drop the tubes he was now carrying into the safety of the kitchen caverns.

The wild gold was watching with great interest. She spread her wings and glided down towards the bowl, coming to land close to Hess and Chris. Chris immediately asked Hess to move away from her, but the bronze refused. *'She trusts me.'* He told Chris.

Chris watched her closely as several other dragons and their riders glided towards the bowl too, keeping their distance from her, but there to offer support to the young pair who had found themselves in such close proximity to the unpredictable wild dragon. As far as Chris knew, she hadn't attacked anyone yet, but everyone was on high alert expecting there to be a first time. He knew Fallaren had expected her to leave Portum before now, he thought she would go back to her wild brethren once she was healed from her injuries. But the small gold had other ideas and she'd settled into her accommodation, showing no signs of leaving.

Now, the Portum dragons arranged themselves in a semi-circle with Chris, Hess and the queen in the centre, ready for action should they be needed. However, the wild gold was showing little interest in Hess, other than acknowledging his presence, she was watching the men moving the tubes. Her head was cocked to one side and each time the tubes clanked together, she made a soft crooning noise.

Bert had been tasked with moving the last tube. As he grasped it and lifted it from the cart, heaving it above the side supports, the queen called. A high, demanding sound issued from her, and she moved towards the cart. Bert dropped the tube he was holding, letting it roll away from him, and backed away into the relative safety of the kitchens.

The rest of the smiths were huddled together behind the big table the cooks used for bread making. Ty had taken charge, ordering as many folk as possible to the storerooms at the back of the kitchens, out of sight of the dragon who was now making her way towards the kitchen entrance, crying and calling. She stopped short of entering the kitchens, crouching and wrapping her tail around her legs, head swaying constantly.

'Hess, can you tell what's wrong with her?' Chris whispered. Hess could only send back confused images from the wild dragon, there was something she wanted.

Fallaren and Narilka appeared in the bowl, both seated on Neldor's neck. Neldor landed close to the queen, refusing to allow his rider or his mate to dismount. He reared back on his haunches, leaving Narilka clinging to Fallaren's waist, and bellowed. The sound rang around the bowl and echoed in the depths of the kitchen caverns.

Everyone had their hands over their ears until the sound died down. But the wild dragon took no notice of the huge bronze, who appeared to be ordering her to step away, to leave. Instead, she lowered her head to look into the kitchens and crooned again.

Fallaren looked around the bowl and spotted Chris and Hess, he waved for them to come closer to Neldor. Slowly, cautiously, Hess approached the leader's dragon. For all Hess was big for his age, Neldor dwarfed him. Hess crept slowly closer until Fallaren could speak to Chris without raising his voice for the whole bowl to hear.

'What's going on?' he demanded in a stage whisper.

Chris could only shrug. 'I don't know,' he replied, 'Hess was feeding, again, and I heard the smiths coming up the trail with these pipes. They were making a lot of noise, loads of people and dragons were watching them. Then she,' he indicated the wild queen, who was now making strange sing song sounds, 'flew down and, well,' he waved an arm, 'this happened.'

Fallaren looked thoughtful. 'Can Hess shed any light on her intentions?'

'No,' Chris sighed, 'I already tried that. He just gives me confused images and says there's something she wants.'

'It couldn't be some -one- could it?' Narilka asked.

'How could it?' Fallaren asked, 'She's no hatchling, she can't bond in the way our dragons have...'

The wild queen moved and Neldor shifted restlessly.

'Can you ask the smiths to come back out?' Chris asked hesitantly.

'Why?' Narilka asked.

'Because she didn't show this much interest until it was just Bert and one of the others out here.' Chris told her.

'You think she's looking for a human?' Narilka asked.

'For breakfast, maybe,' Fallaren said. 'I can't ask these men to risk their lives for some nonsensical idea.'

'Bert!' Chris raised his voice, 'Bert. Can you come back out here please?'

Fallaren whipped round and scowled at Chris, Narilka laid a hand on his arm and murmured something Chris didn't catch. They watched as a very nervous Bert appeared in the cavern opening. The queen's behaviour changed, she became agitated, excitable, extending her head towards Bert, flicking her tongue at him. Bert stood stock still. Chris watched in horrified fascination as the queen inspected his childhood friend.

With the eyes of all the riders, dragons and staff upon him, Bert took a slow, small step towards the golden dragon. She stilled, staring at him, not blinking, not even twitching her tail.

Hess felt it first, then the rest of the dragons let out huge bellows.

Bert's face flushed, he couldn't take his eyes off the queen, who was now moving towards him, lowering her head. As they watched, she nudged against him with her muzzle, the typical manner dragons used to ask their rider to pet them. Tentatively, Bert raised a hand and stroked the soft nose, his face full of wonder and delight.

Chris realised he was watching Bert bonding with a dragon. A wild dragon at that. That which Fallaren had stated was impossible had just happened before the eyes of the whole of Portum. A wild, grown dragon had bonded with a human.

Bert was now a rider, whether he was ready or not, he had got the dragon he craved. Chris sat on Hess's neck, watching Bert and his golden prize.

Bert lifted his head and looked at his friend, 'She says her name is Dannica,' he said.

AFTERWORD

Thank you for reading Volans. If you enjoyed it, please consider leaving me an honest review. Reviews are a great way to help Authors.

I'd love to hear from you with any comments. You can find me on Amazon, Facebook or Instagram, or email me at: kateridleyauthor@gmail.com

If you'd like to know more about Chris and Bert's life before Portum, you can get a free copy of Intus when you sign up to my mailing list

https:// dl.bookfunnel.com/32afzj9j08

BOOKS BY THIS AUTHOR

Portum

Rebelling against the constraints of living underground, a group of teenagers plot their escape.

Two are successful, but now best friends Chris and Bertram are trapped outside, in a strange world full of new dangers.

Rescued by strangers, the boys are taken through a landscape of wide-open spaces and sunshine to a place of relative safety.

And dragons.

Portum follows their adventures as they become accustomed to their new surroundings, making friends and enemies along the way.

ABOUT THE AUTHOR

Kate Ridley is a coffee fuelled, animal loving fantasy fiction writer. Born in York, she lived in North Yorkshire for most of her adult life before relocating to Derbyshire, where she now lives with her partner and two mad rescue dogs.

When she's not writing or cooking up plots, Kate spends her time reading, listening to music, baking, gardening and walking.

Printed in Great Britain
by Amazon